Aandhi

a scenario

Aandhi

a scenario

Gulzar

Translated by
Sunjoy Shekhar

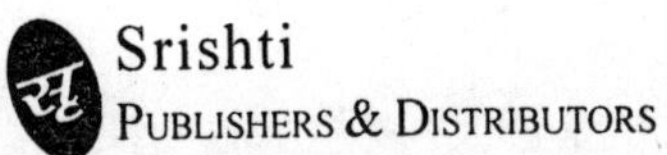

Srishti Publishers & Distributors
N-16, C. R. Park
New Delhi 110 019
srishtipublishers@yahoo.com

First published by Srishti Publishers & Distributors in 2007

ISBN: 81-88575-90-9

Typeset in AGaramond 12pt. by Suresh Kumar Sharma at Srishti

Cover design: Srishti's Art Department

Printed and bound in India

To my colleagues
R. D. Burman & Sanjeev Kumar
the anchor players of
my films.

Foreword

What can be seen is called a scene; and a sequence of scenes is called a screenplay. In English two words are used for it — a screenplay and a scenario. Both are almost alike, but in screenplay the techniques of 'cut', 'dissolve' and others are also written down as directions, which are helpful to the director. Even the time of the 'set' is noted down to denote whether the action takes place in the morning, evening, afternoon or night. These details are required when the director films the screenplay otherwise these technical directions are an unnecessary obstruction in reading. Therefore, a scenario is best suited for a continuous flow of reading, so that it reads like a novel, without any hindrance. This is what is known as a screenplay.

In literature, screenplay is a complete form. The first example that comes to mind is Elia Kazan's screenplay *America America*. This director first wrote the screenplay, published it and then made a film on it. There are many authors in literature who write their novels almost like screenplays. Sharat Chandra's best novels are very close to this form.

One of my motives to present this screenplay is to acquaint the reader with this form and secondly to let the TV and cinema fans know how a novel is adapted into a screenplay. I must admit that I am no expert on adaptation;

another writer or director would, perhaps, create a better screenplay than mine.

The style of writing a screenplay often differs from the original story, and becomes more like an interpretation of the story, the novel or the autobiography. The famous films *Anarkali* and *Mughal-e-Azam* can be cited as examples, which were both derived from the same play. The screenplay of *Devdas* kept changing as many times it was made and in as many languages it was translated into. With the advent of TV there has been a tremendous increase in the demand for screenplays. Screenplays of short stories are being written. A great deal of work is being done on the stories of Ahmad Nadeem Qasmi, Rajinder Singh Bedi, Bhishm Sahni, Munshi Premchand and many others. Several serials are written as screenplays. Since the stipulations of duration of TV films have to be adhered to strictly, the popular stories taken from classical literature have to be abridged sometimes or elaborated as the need may be.

I hope that this attempt of mine will prove to be useful to others as much as their experiences will enrich me and — a new channel might open, a new thought emerge, a new wave rise, perhaps.

— *Gulzar*

Preface

The screenplay of *Aandhi* was written under very interesting circumstances. I was working on the screenplay of *Aandhi* when I happened to meet Kamleshwar regarding the script of another film, which was made under the name *Mausam*. Often we would start talking about one film and end up discussing the other. We had started discussing both the films together. Finally, it was decided that Kamleshwar would write two separate novels on both the stories and I should continue writing the screenplays. This way, I would get some ideas from his novels and my screenplays would unfold some scenes for his novels.

Hence, his novel *Kali Aandhi* and the film *Aandhi* have something in common and yet not quite. In my opinion the attitudes of the characters in the film could not be portrayed in the novel, or let us say, they became different.

The first few scenes were written in Mahabalipuram. Our producer belonged to that place. Then a few were finished in Bhopal, where I had gone to look at a location. But the story did not take off. Ultimately, I completed the script in Delhi's Akbar Hotel, where a waiter called 'J K' served me devotedly, and in his honour I gave the name J K to the hero. And J K knows that!

Another person, J K again, who has taken lots of passion in publishing this book is J K Bose.

One more colleague whom I must mention is my English mentor, translator & friend Sunjoy Shekhar.

— *Gulzar*

The election campaign caught the city by its seams and shook it awake. It dressed it in the colours of a carnival—Gandhi topis worn at rakish angles, paper festoons zigzagging the streets, party flags aflutter in the wind. If you took a walk down the road, you were more likely to be coated in a squirt of dust spewed by the speeding jeeps pressed into election work. Here, a loudspeaker squawked exhorting you to cast your vote in favour of a candidate with a wooden chair as his election symbol. There, a couple of men beseeched you in amplified voices to vote for another candidate who had a bottle for his mascot. The hum and the drum of these campaigning voices shouting in unison their various agendas were overshadowed by the 'hurricane lamp' and the 'bird', the election symbols of Chandersen and Arti Devi. The election was reduced to a contest between the two—Chandersen, the challenger, and Arti Devi, the returning Member of Parliament.

Chandersen took off the stringed offering of marigold flowers and put them on the spotless white dais, tugged on his equally spotless angavastram that dangled so assuringly around his neck—two flowing lengths of liquid white against the earthy colours of his Nehru jacket. He spoke to the sea of supporters gathered in the open maidan. 'Believe you me, I have no desire to contest this election! This morning, when I went to my doctor, neither did he put this on my prescription. And yet, here I am before you, compelled to do so — for the sake of my rights and for the sake of yours.' His voice boomed across the maidan through strategically placed loudspeakers that were to amplify every single syllable of his carefully chiseled speech, a speech that would scrounge for every sympathetic chord in the hearts of its audience, 'Those who think that they can buy the public with a can of kerosene oil or by throwing a fistful of rice in their bags are making a mistake—the public is not for sale. The public will not be sold. The public will not sell its hunger. It will not settle for such a raw deal. I stand here to tell them that the rights of the people will not be sold—

the rights of the people will not be auctioned!' The consummate speaker that Chandersen was, he paused. And, as if on cue, his campaigners who straddled the raised podium, exhorted the gathering, first with a salute to the motherland, and then with a salute to the speaker.

'Hindustan, Zindabad!'

'Chandersen Zindabad!!'

The maidan resonated with the cries. Chandersen masked his pleasure and raised his hands to quieten the endless surge of humanity, 'I stand here before you not to complain. Nor do I have anything against Arti Devi. Need I begrudge her anything? She has, after all, started free kitchens in her election offices: many a starved soul is getting a first square meal—a noble deed, indeed! What can I say to that? Nothing at all. Au contraire, I am happy that the poor people of my city are getting at least one proper meal a day. I have no complaints against her wealth. Nor am I ashamed of my poverty. I can but only say,' he paused, letting his words percolate into every crevice, every chink of his disgruntled audience. And then with the dexterity of a magician who knows that the audience is already his, he repeated, 'I can but only ask — where was she before the elections? In which godowns were these sacks of grain hidden that she has so easily been able to buy off the black market now? Till a few days ago, you couldn't buy a fistful of grain with a pocketful of money. Now, as the elections are approaching, everything has started appearing on the shelves. If I can be made to believe that the people of my city will never know another scarcity, then, believe you me, my brothers and sisters, I would be the first person to queue up to cast my vote in her favour.' He paused again. 'But I know—and you know—the situation is otherwise—this is all a charade, make-believe ... stage-managed to hoodwink you into voting for her.' Another pause, a longer one this time, 'Friends, these 'birds' are no one's friends, they cannot be anyone's friends. They will fly away with your water in their beaks, with your food and your votes in their talons, and they will go and perch on some branch in the distant capital, leaving your hunger unaddressed, your thirst unquenched—forever.'

Arti Devi strode down the stairs of her plush bungalow in a crisp sari and a crisper mood. A pair of dark fashionable glasses masked the wisp of anger in her eyes. She walked into her book-lined office, in the same stride, taking the sunglasses off her eyes. Nothing betrayed the seething rage inside her. She seemed in control. The five party-workers waiting for an audience with her, stood up as she entered the office, diminutive in her presence. She looked at them, asked them to be seated and without as much as wasting another breath said, 'So, the opposition has burnt down our office?' She looked at them, sitting on the edge of her chair, her elbows on the table, her arms crossed.

'Yes, Ma'am, Chandersen has had it burnt down. It is his handiwork.'

'And what makes you say that?' the tone of her voice barely registered a higher decibel.

'His campaigners – they eat with us and sweat with them,' another one grumbled in annoyance.

'Actually, that's where the problem started,' Kamal, the senior-most of those present explained, 'we stopped those freebooters from leeching on us ...Chandersen lent his ears to their story and his tongue went lashing against your free kitchens ...'

'And what a spell he can cast when he speaks !' chimed in another party worker who could not keep the admiration out of his voice, 'when he starts speaking you know how it is ...'

'Yes, I know how it is,' Arti Devi did not take his eyes off the speaker for a moment. He knew he had slipped and fumbled on his way to cover it all up, 'I ... I ... I mean. I mean ... you ... you too are a wonderful orator ... but ... but you are here ... if you had only been there, not a single word would have squeaked out of him. Everyone knows that.'

She tilted her head, interlocked her fingers and her eyes bore into her campaign workers, 'All I hear is Chandersen, Chandersen and just Chandersen in the entire constituency.'

'The biggest factor is—he has plenty of money. The entire business community is backing him.'

Arti Devi turned her gaze on the speaker, 'When you do not have money to throw, you need your wits to live on, Choudhry Sahib!'

'The Aggrawal family is way too influential in Bhopal,' Choudhry tried to explain, 'Old money and an old ally of Chandersen. He owns a number of mills and a number of industries ... annual turnover running into lakhs of rupees—they are the moneybags behind Chandersen.'

'But Lallu Lal had sent word that Aggrawal was going to stand for election,' Arti Devi probed.

'As it is, it is difficult to contain the two of them—what with Chandersen on one side and Gul Sher Khan on the other ... who needs another adversary!' the oldest of the five present, broke his silence.

'The entire business community is united in its support of Chandersen. The Muslims are stauch in their support of Gul Sher Khan,' the other one added.

'We were hoping to get the support of the workers but even that will slip out of our hands,' someone else said, a twinge of fear slipping into his voice.

'Why?' Arti Devi asked.

'If their own mill-owner contests the election they will obviously vote for him— not for anybody else?'

And for the first time Arti Devi betrayed her emotions— irritation crept into her voice, ' What has come over you ... are you out of your minds?' She stood up suddenly, 'Don't the people know ... don't they understand?' She took a measured step, turned, looked at them and asked in earnest, 'Don't they have a newspaper down there?'

'The only important newspaper there,' one of them said, ' is *Watan* and somebody called Giani is the editor.'

Giani, the editor of *Watan*, was sitting across Chandersen's desk in the latter's election office. The silver mane , the tortoise-shell spectacles and the pristine white kurta-pyjamas gave him the look of a man who would brook no nonsense. But Chandersen was a skilful speaker. He had exalted manipulation to an art form. He smiled at Giani, 'Till the elections are over ... don't publish stories about the opposition party on the front page.'

Giani looked at him, 'Are you trying to tell me what I should publish and what I should not?'

'No ... no, no, Gyani ji, don't get me wrong. Publish—by all means publish, but must you publish the stories that which you yourself cannot give much credence to, on the front page ... there are many pages in a newspaper that need to be filled ... tuck them up anywhere ... on the third page ... or on the fourth ... wherever ...'

A party worker walked in with scrolls of artwork. He handed them over to Chandersen, 'Sir, here's the artwork for the main poster ... and the hand bill and this is the order for *Watan* press.'

Chandersen thanked the worker and unrolled the scrolls on his table, 'Here, look at this—the reason I wanted you over,' he said in his eager-to-please voice. 'This is the design for the poster—we will need fifty thousand copies of this printed, and this is the hand bill—one lakh copies of this, and here's the formal order request,' he reached out for his cheque book, made out a cheque, tore it out of the cheque-book and handed it with a flourish to Giani, 'This is merely the advance payment! From now on, all our printing work will be done at your press .'

Giani looked at the cheque in his hand and chortled, emitting two jarring notes of discordant laughter, 'This is not a bribe, is it?'

Chandersen clasped his hands together and with a smile of camaraderie said, 'Must you say so Gianiji? Bribe? ... Oh ... no ... no ... this is just a small give and take between the two us...we need to look after each other, that's all.'

'Fine, I will take care of it,' Chandersen had succeeded in extracting the commitment out of Giani. He looked pleased.

'Fine ... you take care of us before the elections,' Chandersen spoke with assurance, 'And we will take care of you after the elections.'

Lallu Lal, the chief architect of Arti Devi's campaign, picked up the bottle of rum, uncorked it and took a swig of it, sighed and put the bottle back on the table. His co-worker picked up the bottle, examined it and commented, 'It's time you gave up rum Lallu Lalji ... get hooked onto something affordable, brandy maybe ... we have lost this round to Chandersen.'

They were in the campaign office of Arti Devi, dwarfed by giant posters of Arti Devi. Lallu Lal leaned against the table and looked at his co-worker, 'Don't you go raking my wounds man, my hands are tied ... or else I would have taught Chandersen a lesson or two ...'

'Your hands are tied ... how do you mean?'

'I would have given that Chandersen the bitter taste of his own medicine ... but alas ... our Arti Devi is an apostle of Mahatma Gandhi ... she will not lift a little finger against anyone, leave alone raise a hand.'

It was then that another campaign worker walked in, tremedously agitated, with a copy of *Watan* in his hand, 'Here have a look ... see Lallu Lalji ... Chandersen is all over ... front page ... centrespread...ads all over ... slowly but steadily he has spread himself all over the press.'

'Bhaiye ... why just the press ... Chandersen has spread like a cancer all over the election scene. Between him and Gul Sher Khan everything is decided: on one side is Chandersen with his hand deep in Agarwal's pockets, and with the entire business community behind him, and on the other, Gul Sher Khan has the Muslim votes in his pocket ... what are we to do?'

'I would suggest that you ask Arti Devi to come over for

a few days ... once she is around ... attends a few meetings ... the winds will change.'

Lallu Lal snorted an agreement and got up from his chair, 'That I know ... but who the hell is going to sit down for her lectures and her moralizing ... for her do's and her don't's ... don't do this ... that is not the way it should be done ... walk on the straight and narrow path ... man ... this is a different age and people listen to a different reasoning ... if you stick to the straight and narrow you will never even reach your home, forget reaching the parliament.'

'Come on Lallu Lalji, who on earth is asking you to tell her anything at all ... just have her come over here ... everything else will fall into place.'

The idea had an irresistible appeal. Lallu Lal mulled it over and then looked at the other man, 'but where is she going to stay when she comes over here?'

'The election office has been razed to the ground...why don't we book her into a good hotel?'

The jeep skimmed through the city and screeched to a halt outside a red-brick colonial hotel. Lallu Lal stepped out of the jeep, a khadi jhola slung across his shoulder, a swagger in his steps and confidence in his face. He cantered to the front office of the hotel. Lallu Lal, like always, oozed attitude. He leaned across the front office desk and asked the suit-and-tie, 'Bhaiyye, where is the Manager?'

The suit-and-tie looked at his watch, 'Should be in the garden.'

Lallu Lal looked amused, 'Why, does the watch tell him when to take a walk in the garden?'

'No ... not a walk actually ... he is getting some work done.'

'Well then, send for him.'

'You need to book a room?'

'Not a room, a number of rooms. Why don't you just go and fetch the Manager.'

'Sir, he is in the garden. You may meet him there.'

Lallu Lal turned to go, then stopped and asked, 'What's his name?'

'JK.'

'JK? He is the manager, right?'

'Yep ... the Manager as well as the Managing Director.'

Lallu Lal swung out from there.

JK was on his knees, weeding out unwanted growth.

'Bhaiyye,' the strangeness of Lallu Lal's voice startled him. He turned. The soft light of the afternoon sun filtering through the green canopy of leaves highlighted the silver-grey of his temples. JK got up.

'So, you are the Manager of the hotel?'

JK stood in his unbuttoned sleeves and looked at Lallu Lal. He brushed the dirt off his hands, 'Yes Sir, how may I help you?'

'Oh ... it is okay ... you may clean up first ... and then we can talk.'

JK looked at the his hands. Blotches of caked mud clung to his palms. He moved towards the garden-tap and began to wash his hands, ' What is it that you need?'

'Arre Bhaiye, what else will one want from you ... a place to stay in the hotel...but in this case a lot of space ... just get the South Wing vacated. It will do.'

'How many rooms do you want?' JK wiped his hands with his handkerchief and began to roll down his sleeves and cuffed them at the links.

'Arre bhaiye, must you count your blessings. You know how it is with politicians on their campaign trails—they carry their offices with them. The leader will take up residence on the upper floor, the office will spring open in the space below.'

'From when would you be needing them?' JK picked up his jacket.

'From today! The whole hoard would be swarming down tomorrow.'

'And who may this leader of yours be?'

'Arti Devi!'

'Arti Devi?' JK spoke the syllables of the name, a number of emotions criss-crossed his face, 'she ... she is going to stay here.'

'Yes! She is the leader of the masses. She will stay where the masses are. You have a problem with that?'

'No Sir, why should I have a problem with it.' But JK looked visibly disturbed.

'You are in a win-win situation—her stay here will lend glamour to your hotel.'

If JK heard Lallu Lal, it certainly did not register with him. He was on a different plane—the mention of Arti Devi had opened up something within him, 'This ... this Arti Devi—isn't she the one whose election symbol is the bird?'

'Bhaiyye,' Lallu Lal looked at him in disbelief, 'who else would dare fly so high in the sky?'

The deafening whirr of the helicopter rotors refused to dampen the enthusiasm of the reception committee led by Lallu Lal, that had gathered in the scorching heat of an Indian afternoon to welcome Arti Devi. Arti Devi stepped out of the helicopter even before the rotors became silent. The crowd went ecstatic at the sight of her. She was garlanded, felicitated and the sky was rent with chants of 'Arti Devi Zindabad'. Her motorcade left for the hotel en route roads lined with supporters chanting, 'Arti Devi Zindabad! Long live Arti Devi!'

The words bounced off the simmering hot roofs of the convoy, echoed and re-echoed in the numerous lanes and by-lanes of the town.

JK stood on the balcony of his hotel room, dressed in an immaculately tailored beige suite. From where he stood, he could see a crush of people swarming the hotel entrance to get a glimpse of the leader, of Arti Devi. The procession arrived, and amidst much fanfare Arti Devi was ushered inside the hotel. JK stood there, simply watching her.

With a clutch of marigold garlands in her hand, Arti Devi stepped into the South Wing of the hotel, the place which was to officiate as her campaign headquarters. Campaign posters stared at her from almost every wall. She did not seem pleased though, 'What's this ... they should have been in Hindi.'

She moved in, looked around. The rooms looked stark to her, 'What's this ... are there no beds in this hotel?'

'I have had them removed!' Lallu Lal was ready with an explanation.

'Why?'

'Bec...bec...because ...' Lallu Lal begun telling her why but then he decided against it, 'this ... this is not where you will be staying ... your lodgings have been prepared upstairs ... come ... I ... I shall take you there.'

Lallu Lal held open the door to Arti Devi's room and the delicate smell of sandalwood wafted out. A bunch of sandalwood incense sticks glowed ember on the bedside table. Arti Devi looked at Lallu Lal, 'Sandalwood incense sticks! Who put them here?'

From the expression on her face, Lallu Lal could not make out whether the fragrance pleased her or incensed her. So, Lallu Lal washed his hands off the entire thing, 'I have no idea Ma'am. Appears to be the ingenuity of the hotel staff.'

'That's really thoughtful of them ... I love them.' And then, as she turned she caught glimpse of the *surahi*, the earthen water pitcher. She moved towards it and sat with her legs crossed on the recliner, 'Someone out here is well aware of my taste ... a quaint surahi instead of a modern flask ... something that these days you do not find even in your own homes.'

The conversation was certainly taking a turn that Lallu Lal was not liking. He excused himself, 'Ar...rr ...you must be tired ... you need to rest, why don't I finalize your programme with Gursaran.' And saying this Lallu Lal beat a hasty retreat.

A tired and distraught Lallu Lal was taking off his slippers when Gursaran walked into the room. Lallu Lal called out after him, 'Arey Gursaran.'

'What is it Lallu Maharaj?'

'Bhaiyye, knock some sense into Deviji's head. Well ... if this is going to be her attitude, then she can forget about winning this election!'

'Why, what's happened?'

'Arre, nothing can happen if she carries such an attitude? To win an election you need to roll on a bed of thorns? And your Deviji—she is not even prepared to sit on the floor. I had it all planned: all sorts of people would be walking in and out of this place the whole day—and they would see her sitting on the floor like 'them' commoners; wearing simple cotton suits like 'them' commoners ... and these are the people who go out and talk ... just imagine for a moment what they would have said ... that Arti Devi is just like them ... and that is how you connect with the people ... that is how you build up a campaign ... I had it all planned, but Deviji ...'

'But where is she?'

'Oh ... inside ... looking at her bed ... go ... talk to her ... and tell her that I am right.'

'Don't tell her what is right or what is wrong—she knows better than you or I.' Lallu Lal had touched a sympathetic note in Gursaran. He rambled on, 'Once I asked her to ride the train ... but she outrightly refused ... she thought it a waste of time. Preferred the plane ... said she spends her own money.'

Lallu Lal sighed, 'Yeah ... she's a rich man's daughter ... if she will not spend his money, who will? Fine, let her do as she desires. . .a man can only do so much ...'

Thoroughly unhappy, he walked out of the room.

When Amrit, the assistant manager of the hotel, walked into JK's office, he found him reclining on his chair, his eyes closed.

'Sir, sir,' he called out for JK a couple of times before JK opened his eyes.

'Sorry...sorry!' JK seemed tired. It worried Amrit.

'Sir, you don't look too well, sir. You have been working quite late into the night. Why don't you retire to the cottage. If need be, I shall come over ...'

'I am okay ... okay ... what's bothering you ... come on, out with it?' JK sensed that Amrit had something pressing on his mind.

'Sir, that Lallu Babu from the South Wing ... he had come over ... he wants to display Arti Devi's posters in the front windows.'

'There we go again,' JK sighed, 'Refuse it. Tell them in no uncertain terms that we will have no political activity in the hotel. Whatever propaganda they want to do, they will have to do outside the hotel premises.'

JK picked up his pen to clear a few pending files.

A man from housekeeping walked in with a bouquet of flowers in his hand. JK looked at him, 'Finally, you got those flowers ... keep them here,' he looked at Amrit, 'Amrit, take these flowers to her room personally.'

'Whose room, Sir?'

'Hers ... Arti Devi's.' JK looked at the flowers, touching them.

'Sir, sign on it,' Amrit presented a card, 'This will make it more personal.'

JK toyed with the idea, but decided against it, 'No Amrit, in fact, don't say it's from the Manager. Just say it is from Hotel Ashiana.'

Amrit picked up the bouquet and left the room. JK was entombed in his own loneliness.

Arti Devi answered the doorbell. Amrit stood there with the bouquet of flowers. He proffered the flowers to her and wished her.

She was bowled over by the flowers, ' Oh! How beautiful! Who has sent them?'

'They are from the hotel ... ma'am.'

'Someone here seems to know my taste pretty well. Put them in the vase over there, please.'

And Arti Devi walked back to her desk and immersed herself in her work.

JK flicked the butane lighter and lit his after-dinner cigarette, blew a puff of smoke, got up from the dining table and sat down on the sofa. Binda, the old family retainer, cleared the table and then came back with a bowl of dessert and handed it over to JK.

'What is it?'

'I made some kheer today.'

'Kheer ... today ... all of a sudden?'

'I saw Mem Sa'ab today,' there was a faraway look in his eyes, as if he was transported to a different era, 'so I thought of it ... she always loved kheer.'

'Mem Sa'ab?'

'I mean *bahurani*!'

'*Bahu ... Rani*?' JK chuckled, 'What has come over you now Binda? You always used to call her your *bitiya* then.'

Binda was trying hard to control his emotions, his voice quivered when he spoke, 'So many years have come between then and now ... so many things have changed ... so many things have snapped.'

'Do bonds snap with years?'

'The bond with this house at least has snapped.'

When JK spoke, the voice seemed to come from far away, 'Don't know from where the bond has snapped or where it's still linked.'

JK stared into the bowl of kheer, pondering over the past years. He put a spoonful into his mouth, 'Have you met her?'

'No!'

'Why?'

'I needed to ask you.'

'You needed to ask me ... you need my permission to meet her ... why ... you of all the people ... you have helped raise her ... she grew up in front of you ... you have by far more right over her than I ... you don't need my permission to meet her?'

Binda was overwhelmed with emotions, 'I ... I saw her ... her ... my bitiya ... from a distance ... but ... but I saw her ... after ages ... I ... I wanted to call out after her ... but ... but she was surrounded with so many important people ... she ... she has become so grown-up ... that ...'

Binda looked away, moved towards the wall to hide his emotions. A silence engulfed the room. The past had suddenly, without any warning, descended upon the two men.

'You should take a bowl of this kheer to her—you had made it for her after all.'

'There will be so many people out there. Nobody would let me near her.'

'Why won't they let you in? Go ... she is hosting a dinner in the hotel garden. Ask any hotel bearer to take you there,' he paused, 'and listen, if she is with important looking people, then it would be better not to crowd her ... in that case, ask the bearer to take it to her.'

Binda looked at JK, a bundle of mixed emotions and with unsure steps, he walked out of the room.

If you were to judge by the smiles on the faces of the workers and campaigners, the party hosted by Arti Devi on the lawns of Hotel Aashina was turning out to be a great success. Lallu Lal sat at a table with two other campaign workers. He drained the last drop from his bottle and excused himself from the table and moved towards a bearer, 'Excuse me,' he said handing over his empty bottle to the man, 'would you please get me the medicine for my kidneys, please.'

'What?' The man looked clueless.

'Arre ... bhaiye ... go to the bar and get some rum for me ...'

'Got it!' the man laughed as understanding dawned on him.

'Understood ... then go ... go fast!'

Binda came into the garden with the bowl of kheer. He paused as he saw the party in progress. He was unsure of himself. The more he looked at the people in the garden, the more hesitant he became. Finally, he gathered enough courage to ask a waiter, 'Where can I find Arti Devi?'

'She hasn't come in yet! She is upstairs.'

'In her room?'

'Yes, some important people are visiting her.'

The waiter moved away. As Binda turned to leave, Arti Devi walked into the garden flanked by a few hangers-on. They took leave of her and she turned to enter the garden when her eyes fell on Binda—a face from her past. Binda kept looking at her, still uncertain, still apprehensive.

'Binda Kaka, you here,' she bent down to touch his feet and seek his blessing.

And that removed all apprehensions, all fear from Binda. He knew it was his *bitiya* who was in front of him. He was touched.

'No, beti, no ... don't do that,' he did not want to let her out of his sight even for once, 'May you live long! How have you been?'

'I am well, but ... but what brings you here?'

'I ... stay here ... with Sahib. Sahib is the Manager of this hotel. It's been four years now.'

It was that strange kind of news, the type that demanded too many questions and left too few answers, that brought in joy and sorrow, happiness and sadness in equal measures and in such quick succession that when they left, your face was left as expressionless as it had been when you had first heard it.

'Now that will stop me from wondering who it is over here who knows me so well?'

'Sahib has not met you?' Binda found it hard to believe.

'He ... he is here ... is he?'

'Yes, at the bungalow ... right behind the hotel block . . he has just finished his dinner,' then he looked at the bowl of kheer in his hand and once again became unsure of himself, ' I made this kheer for you, I thought maybe ...'

She took the bowl from his hand and gave it to her aide, 'Have this brought to my room!' and then turned towards Binda Kaka, 'Kaka, I will have it later ...'

Binda turned to go. He kept looking at him.

'Kaka!'

Binda turned.

'Come again to meet me. I am going to be here for a few days.'

'Yes, yes, I shall!'

She kept looking at Binda as he trotted away, old but sure in his steps, towards JK's bungalow.

JK, comfortably ensconced in his chair, in the quiet of his room, was wrapped in his thoughts. A part of him stayed in the past, in memories that he wondered had ever been his own. The doorbell throbbed, demanding that he pull himself together. He looked at the door and slowly walked to answer it. He opened the door and, without warning, his past trundled in. On the other side of the threshold stood Arti Devi, a present from the past. JK saw his entire life reflected in the twin pools of her coal-black eyes. They kept looking at each other: eternities condensed in those moments.

'Just the same,' she spoke, her eyes still riveted on his face, 'You haven't changed a bit.'

'A ... a,' his lips quivered under the weight of all those past years, 'a ... bit weak but ...'

'Weak ... no,' the words came steadily but haltingly, '... no way ... you were never weak, a bit thinner, yes .'

'Thinner?' he chortled, ' Aged, more like it. See the grey in my hair.'

'Must be loving it! You so loved dusting your hair grey even then.'

'You remember everything still?'

'Have you forgotten anything? I thought of you when I saw that surahi in the room, but did not think that you would be here ... only when I saw Binda ...'

They continued to stand at the threshold of each other's life.

'Will you not ask me to come in?'

'Ya ... ya .. do . .do come in.' He moved away from the doorway.

Arti Devi walked in, holding the door, gingerly stepping into another time and space, looking around, letting it all seep in.

'This ... this moustache ... when did that spring up on your face ?' She was not looking at him, the moustache had been bothering her.

'About a few years ago,' his hand went up to his moustache instinctively as if he too had become aware of its presence on his upper lip with Arti Devi's words, 'Never did like them, did you?'

'Is that what made you ...?'

'No ... no ... just like that!'

And he laughed and she joined in his laughter, the two laughter becoming one another's shadow.

She took another tentative step into the house, 'So clean and tidy—who keeps the house in such order?'

'Binda!'

'Oh!'

She crossed the length of the living room. Her eyes wanted to ask him a number of questions, her ears wanted to hear the answers to all those unasked questions. But none were forthcoming. And she was finding it difficult to contain herself. 'Mannu—she's not around?'

'In Shimla,' the words took time to form on his lips, 'she stays in a boarding school.'

A silence like a mist formed between the two of them and then his voice came through the mist, 'Shall we ... go out ... into the garden?'

'Eh ... haan!'

They stepped out into the garden, sat across each other on wicker chairs, separated by the length of a coffee table—but the table stretched endlessly in their imagination. The misty silence once again swooped down on them and made them its prisoners. She picked up an old issue of a discarded magazine from the table and began to leaf through it aimlessly. He kept looking at her— numerous words took shape on his lips but they disappeared much before they could find his tongue. All he could hear himself asking was, 'Will you have something? Some tea, maybe coffee?'

'Coffee!' she said without looking up from the magazine and then suddenly, she remembered something, looked up at him, 'But doesn't coffee bother you at night time?'

'No ... not any more,' he lied and called for the old manservant, 'Binda!'

'Aaya Saheb!!' Binda could hear him even in his sleep and he came running in. His happiness knew no bounds when he saw Arti Devi sitting there, 'Arre bitiya ji, you ... you are here.'

'What about some coffee, Kaka?'

'Of course, why not,' there was nothing he could refuse the visitor. He turned to go and then paused, 'but for Sahib, coffee at this time in the night is ...'

'... not good for him ... isn't it?' Arti Devi completed Binda's sentence. 'I knew it,' she looked at a very sheepish JK now that he was caught. Arti Devi turned towards Binda. For now, she had stepped into the role of the lady of the house and she reveled in it. She had taken possession, she was in charge, 'Kaka, brew him some ginger tea, the way you always used to do.'

'Yes! Yes! That's better!' the words tumbled off Binda's excited and happy lips, 'See Sahib, bitiya ... she ... she hasn't forgotten a thing ... I'll just be back with the coffee and the ginger tea.'

And Binda ran into the kitchen—the two of them together was what he had always imagined them to be.

Arti Devi's eyes followed him till he disappeared inside

the house and then she slowly turned away from the door, her eyes on her magazine but her mind clearly someplace else. For a moment, the monotonous chirping of the crickets stayed the only sound of the night between the two of them. And then JK's voice was heard, an octave higher, 'Binda's very thrilled today!'

'Hoon ...' her voice came from a distant past. She got up from her chair ... the magazine, still rolled, in her hands, she walked past JK, 'so many years have crept between you and I ... am meeting you after ... what ... some nine years...nine years have gone past us, have they not?'

He just sat there, looking at her, letting her words caress his face, moisten his eyes.

'I had returned home once!' her voice had a strange quality to it, a mix of sadness and regret, 'but perhaps too late ... You were long gone! Been to the hotel—where you worked as the assistant manager. You were gone from there too.'

'I keep reading about you. Somewhere, I read that your tonsils had been operated upon.'

'Haan ... our lives are open books ... anyone can peep into them ... know about them ... nothing can remain your own ... everything is out there in the open.'

'Are you not happy with this life? Quite successful ...

you've have come a long way!'

JK's concern echoed within her, albeit for a moment—was she happy with this life? She did not find any answer forthcoming. She smiled sadly, and then moved towards him, 'Didn't get to hear anything about you,' she moved closer to him.

'I am trailing a bit too far behind!' The years had lessened the pain but had not taken away his trade-mark self-deprecating humour.

Binda silently came in with the tea things and was gone before he could be seen.

Arti Devi sat back in her chair and pulled the tea things towards herself, 'Here, let me ... I will make it.'

She began pouring the tea into the cups. 'Don't you write any more?'

'Rarely...a bit now and then.'

He kept looking at her, the way her nimble fingers moved about the tea things—he had always liked the way she looked when she poured him tea.

Many years ago, that was the sight he woke up to. Everyday.

Arti Devi sat, looking gorgeous in her red-border-polka-dotted sari, next to a sleeping JK. She always had her bath much before JK even stirred in his bed. And her hair was still wet from the bath and hung down traced a wild arc to her waist. Binda brought in the tea things. She put her hand on the tea-pot and immediately withdrew it.

'Steaming ... ah ...' she screamed.

'Ji. . quite,' Binda moved out of the bedroom.

Arti Devi poured the tea in the cup, stirred in the sugar and then looked at JK who was lying on his stomach, oblivious to his surroundings, lost in sleep. Arti Devi smiled to herself and then, very tentatively, took hold of his hand and maneuvered his middle finger into the hot cup of tea.

'Ouch!!!' JK shot upright, instinctively sucking his scalded finger. He glared at Arti Devi, nonplussed.

She was unfazed and looked at him through her beautiful innocent eyes, 'Is the sugar to your taste?'

'Is that any way to wake anyone up!' he grumbled trying to shake the pain off his finger.

'No ... not to wake you up but to find out if the sugar in the tea's okay,' she said, 'I tried to wake you up twice before. What more can a person do?'

'Why ... couldn't you simply have switched the radio on,' he yawned.

'That happens only in the movies, not in real life.'

JK was now fully awake. He gazed at her as he sipped his tea. An impish glee crept into his eyes as he put the tea cup down on the table and took hold of her hand, 'What is this ... on your hand ... here ... Let me see!'

'Where?' she was still innocent to his ploy. But JK was enjoying himself. He played on, 'Here! See!!' JK tried to dip her hand into the still steaming cup of tea, but she had by then become wise to the idea. She tried to pull her hand away and in the ensuing fracas the entire tea pot spilled on his feet.

That was many years ago. Life has an uncanny way of recreating past events. JK was disturbed by the memory, ruffled by the thought that they could have been together. When he came back to the present he was so jolted that he upset the tea-table and only somehow managed to stem the tea from spilling onto them. The chirping of the cricket once again filled the silence between them.

'What's the matter?' she asked him.

'Nothing ... nothing at all!' he tried to smile his embarrassment away.

She handed him his cup of tea. She kept looking at him till he took a sip, 'Is the sugar to your taste!'

He looked at her. There was this hint of shared mischief itching to crawl out of the corners of her eyes.

'Yes.'

'Do you remember how I used to wake you up in the mornings to ask you about the sugar?'

They were both haunted by the same memories.

'I do.' He kept his eyes lowered on the rim of the cup.

'And the time when the entire table toppled over on your feet. It was you who were responsible for it and you blamed me for it.'

They had travelled the years and were now in the past, reliving the moments that had once bonded them together.

Haan ... haan ... I love spilling boiling water on my feet, yes of course!' he was nursing the scalded foot.

'Stop it . . .It's just water!' she was trying to put some ointment on it.

'Why don't you go fetch some red hot embers and brand my feet with it. Some day I am going to do just that to you... if

you don't fry like dal ...!!'

'Weren't you the one to say revolutionaries can walk on fire,' she loved rubbing him the wrong way, 'What has changed now?'

'No one jumps into fire without any reason. I was twelve years old when I took a bullet for the sake of my party.'

'Then why are you against the party these days?'

'The party was a revolutionary party those days! We fought for the revolution!' He was outraged at the suggestion that there could be any comparison between present-day party politics and the political ideals underlying the freedom struggle.

'Even now, we are fighting for the same cause.'

'Yes, indeed! These strikes and these satyagrahas—you think you can usher in a revolution with these?'

'So far they have done so, yes.'

'Now don't you start arguing with me unnecessarily. Just because you have read politics for your ... what ... BA and MA ... let me be ... let go off my leg ... let go,' he pulled his leg away from her. By then, she had already applied the ointment on his foot and calf.

'You sure took a long time to pull your foot away,' she would not let go off any chance to tease him.

The tease worked and he got agitated, not able to take his wife's innocent dig, he began to rumble, 'Now, hear ... hear ...

this ... this is politics! This is what I call politics! That is why I hate it!' She was enjoying every bit of it and laughed. She got up, walked to the wardrobe while he carried on with his tirade, 'As far as I am concerned, where honesty doesn't work, nothing works.'

Arti Devi took out a towel from the wardrobe and threw it at him, 'Now, you get ready fast, I have to go.'

'Now, where do you have to go today?'

'To my parents'.'

'More council work come up? Again?' He picked up his toothpaste and brush.

'A little. Father's. I shall go, wrap it all up and be back soon.' She looked at him endearingly.

He uncapped his toothbrush and squeezed some paste on it, 'Just can't wait for you to be a mother—then we'll see whose council holds sway—your father's or your son's.'

She blushed at the thought and then pushed him into the bathroom, 'Now, get going.'

'Arti,' he bounced back from the bathroom, leaned against the doorframe and said through a spray of toothpaste foam, 'I was thinking, what if it is not a son but a daughter. Then?'

'Uph!' she was losing patience, 'Hurry up, Daddy must be waiting!'

He moved into the bathroom and then remembered

something and chuckled at the memory and came out again, 'I will tell you a very interesting story ... You know when I was twelve years old ...'

'You will forever stay just twelve years old,' she was at the end of her tether now, and dragged him into the bathroom.

Arti Devi walked into the booklined office of her father, resplendent in a white silk sari with red border.

'Late again,' Arti's father reprimanded her. 'Don't you remember we are to go for the meeting?'

'He got late leaving for his office, Daddy,' she got busy with the files, leafing through its contents.

'What has his leaving got to do with your arriving here?' Mr Bose, her father, had no patience with the petty demands of domestic life. He had not raised his daughter to while her life away in the discharge of trivial household chores.

'Oh ... I need to make sure he has his breakfast or else he will skip it and run to the hotel!' she looked up briefly from the file at the father.

'Why, isn't Binda at home?'

'Binda's there ... but it is I who has to ensure that he has his breakfast.'

'Why? You feed him with your own hands? Is he a baby?' The father did not like the images Arti's words conjured. He took the glasses off his eyes and looked at Arti, confounded. Arti chuckled.

'No, Daddy ... not a baby ... but like a baby. And like a kid, he constantly needs attention.'

JK walked out of the bathroom with his tousled wet head of hair, a white wet towel dangling around his neck fumbling with the string of his pyjamas. Arti Devi was busy in the kitchen, fixing breakfast.

'Arti. I did try a lot. Sincerely, I did. But I just can't seem to get it in. Put this in.'

'Uh oh! This drawstring of yours! It's a nuisance,' she put the bowl on the kitchen top and moved towards the refrigerator to take out a few eggs, 'you can climb a mountain on a string but you can't string your pyjamas on your own!'

She moved towards the stove and lit a flame. He followed her around.

'Listen . . .climbing mountains and stringing pyjamas are two entirely very different things. I can shoot a goal on the hockey field but I cannot thread a needle but that does not mean. . .'

'Here ... Give ... give me the pyjama,' she pulled the pyjamas out of his hand, 'you can't do a thing.'

'Now, don't you go saying I can't do anything,' he protested, 'I can pen such poems that will swoon you into marrying me all over again. Shall I recite one?'

'No, no ... there's much work to be done.'

'Work??? What work can interest you more than my poems?'

'Stringing your pyjamas for example!' She baited him with those kohl-lined innocent eyes. She was done with the pyjamas.

'Radheyshyam!' he despaired, 'My poems and these pyjamas!!! You have ruined the entire image! Here give them back to me.'

He snatched the pyjamas from her hands. And her unbridled, uninhibited laughter filled the room as she broke an egg into the bowl. Something unexplained lurked behind that laughter of hers.

A few moments later, Binda walked into the kitchen.

'Binda Kaka!!'

Binda turned to find her taking out a piece of paper from the folds of her sari.

'What's it?' Binda Kaka looked at her.

Arti handed the piece of paper to him, an air of conspiracy about her, 'Quick ... have this telegram sent!'

'Telegram? To whom?' Binda could not fathom what was happening.

'To your Sahib in the hotel. He's working the afternoon shift. He will get it within two hours.' She smiled.

'Arrey Sahib is sitting right there in the hall,' Binda laughed, unwilling to believe that she was serious, 'Must you send him a telegram?'

Arti put a finger to her lips to hush him, 'Shh... he will hear you. He should not get to know. Now please hurry, Kaka!'

Binda could not say no to her, however strange her request may have been.

An immaculately dressed JK walked into the front office of his hotel. Amrit was manning the front desk at that moment. JK smiled at him, 'Hello Good Morning!'

And he picked up the phone. Before he could dial a number, Amrit handed him a telegram.

'What's this?'

'There's a telegram for you!'

He tore the telegram and read it.

'Oh ... no ...'

Amrit was getting concerned. He kept looking at him, solicitous, 'What's the matter? JK?'

JK burst into peals of laughter, 'Oh! Yaar! My wife has got a classic sense of humour!' JK just could not stop laughing. He waved the telegram at Amrit, 'I am going to become a father.'

'You are going to become a father!' Amrit grabbed his hands and pumped in his congratulations, 'Congratulations! Yaar Congratulations!

'Thanks!' JK was convulsing with mirth. Amrit was bewildered—he could not see anything to laugh about in the news.

'But what's so funny?'

'This!' JK waved the telegram in Amrit's face, 'This ... this telegram ....! She could have broken the news this morning ... I was all the time around her ... at home ... but no ... she prefers to wire me a telegram!'

Amrit got the humour and he joined JK in his laughter. And then suddenly, JK stopped laughing. Amrit looked at him. JK put on a very serious face and looked at Amrit, 'Do me a favour. Send a telegram on my behalf ... It should congratulate her right at the outset and then say that I will be coming home by about nine-thirty tonight ... and that she should have the son ready to meet the father by then.'

Amrit was getting the hang of JK's sense of humour by now.

He could not suppress his laughter, 'Hey! What do you think, the baby will be born in a day? It takes nine months to give birth to a baby, doesn't it?'

JK was reading and re-reading the telegram. He unfolded and folded it once again and then looked at Amrit with pride, 'You don't know my wife yaar! She can do a month's work in a day and she will do it just like that, in a jiffy.'

The nursery in the house came to life. JK knew of no greater joy. Nor could he wait for her daughter to grow up. He had filled the room with all sorts of toys—anything and everything that arrested his eyes on shelves of the toyshops in town found its way into his daughter's room—toys that the infant were too young to even grapple with. And he lay next to his wife, playing with the toys. Arti Devi kept looking at him, the baby girl between them.

'Have you thought of a name for your daughter?'

He looked at her then looked away and thought for long and then rolled the four syllables out on his tongue, 'Ma-no-ra-ma!'

It met with instant rejection, 'Chhi!! It reminds me of that fatso ... no ... I don't like it!'

'Don't worry ... We shall condense it to Man ...'

'That's too short,' her objection was instant.

'Fine then we shall say it twice ... Man ... Man ...' he was not going to give it up so easily.

'Oh, that sounds like somebody ringing a bell.'

He laughed.

'Then ... then we shall call her Mannu!'

'Mannu ... Mannu!!' Arti Devi's voice could be heard in the room where Mannu was lost in a world populated by her toys. She was now four years old. JK was sprawled on his stomach on the sofa, getting his back massaged by Binda. He was trying to gather a few thoughts to string them into a poem. Mannu did not hear the mother calling. JK looked up at her, 'Mannu ... Mannu ... Mama's calling for you.'

'O ... ho ... nothing in this house can be done without me,' little Mannu did not like to be pried away from her world even if it was by her mother. She got up to go to the mother.

JK stumbled on the right words for his thoughts. He was ecstatic, 'Binda ... what a line ...'

Arti Devi entered the room at that very moment. She sighed when she saw the condition the room was in. She started to put the room in order.

'Arti,' JK did not look up from his piece of paper, 'Listen to this ... I have penned a poem.'

Arti stopped whatever she was doing, turned around to look at him—her arms filled with Mannu's toys. 'So, here you are writing a poem.' And she let out a laugh. Her laughter resonated in the room.

JK looked at her, ' What's there to laugh about in this?'

She moved closer towards JK, an amused look on her face, an impish glee in her eyes, 'You look like a tube of a toothpaste ... he is squeezing you from out there and from here the poem is frothing forth.'

Even Binda could not help but burst into laughter.

JK turned, looked at Binda, 'Binda Kaka ... you please go.' Binda left.

'You have spoilt my entire image.' The applause had been denied the child. He sulked.

The child needed to be placated. Arti Devi cuddled towards him, 'Here ... recite!'

'No ... no ... I am not in the mood, ' he was feeling rebuffed.

'Fine, don't,' she snatched the piece of paper and began to read it, 'I will read it myself.'

She was enjoying herself and liked what she was reading,

'Wah ... Wah ... very romantic.'

That was all the appreciation JK needed. He started off, 'Arti ... I was this romantic even when I was just twelve years old!'

Arti Devi put on her I-believe-you-if-you-say-so-face, 'Really???'

Before JK could say anything Mannu came running in, 'Babuji ... Babuji ... let's

go and get a cake for my birthday!'

JK smiled indulgently, 'Mannu ... if you want to have a cake, it is not necessary that it be your birthday ... I shall get you one.'

'No ... no ... now ... right now,' his daughter became difficult.

'But right now ... I am busy.'

'No ... no ... now ...right now.' Mannu refused to understand.

'If you keep throwing tantrums like these I shall have you sent to a hostel,' JK threatened.

That was all in the past now. That was a life of which she was once an inseparable part. That was then, this was now. Arti Devi pulled herself together.

'When did you send Mannu to the hostel?'

'About three years now. She scribbles such wonderful letters that I can hear her lisp in them.'

'She must be ten years old now.'

'Yes, she will be completing eleven in December.'

Silence had now begun to dot their conversation—theirs had been a shared past, the dots connected by silence.

She touched the teapot.

'It's grown cold. Shall I ask him to brew a fresh pot?'

'No, I better go now,' she stood up. JK picked up her shawl that hung on the wicker chair and he very delicately put it over her shoulders. She kept looking at him, sensing his proximity even after all those years. They began to walk out of JK's house. She stopped at the wicket door and looked at him.

'Come, I shall see you off to your room.'

'It is better if you don't. I don't want people to know about us.'

'Yes, yes,' he took a couple of steps backwards, 'yes, yes ... that's what I had thought this very morning. That is why I didn't come to meet you. But ...' the unspoken words hung in the air ... he let the words be and hurriedly said, 'it's okay.'

She looked at him, at the few moments that they had stolen from time and she walked away from the past back into the present.

A very distraught Chandersen walked into the election office. He seemed to be preoccupied. Things were not turning out the way he had planned.

'Kartar, have you taken the court's declaration for publishing our paper?'

Kartar, the party worker, showed him the block of the masthead for the newspaper that Chandrasen was planning to launch.

'Yes, Sir, everything is ready. And today even the setters have sent us the block of *Zamana*.'

'*Zamana!!*' Chandrasen rolled the name on his tongue ... He liked the sound of it, 'It's a nice name! *Zamana!*' he paused, and then appraised the masthead block, 'I have spoken to Gyani, but I don't trust him. These newspaperwallahs suffer from a disease called intelligence—they obsess over everything ... the day Gyani messes things up that very day we shall launch our own newspaper.'

'But we will need lots of funds for that. And where will

we get so much money from?'

'Let's see, I will talk to Aggrawal about it. If we get newsprint from his paper mills... then it shouldn't be difficult?'

'No, Sir, then there is no problem.'

Chandersen ruminated over the whole thing. A passing notion caught his fancy, 'Gyani's newspaper—*Watan*—who supplies newsprint for his paper?'

'Sir, as far as I know, it comes from Aggrawal too.'

A devilish gleam crept into Chandersen's eyes and stayed there, 'If that is the case, Gyani will not cause us any concern.'

Chandersen was once again at the helm of his affairs, 'Now all that needs to be seen is who gets to be the front page news—Arti Devi or I?'

Arti Devi was on her way to address a gathering of her supporters. She sat in the car, her eyes hidden behind large, dark sunglasses, her head covered by the pallu of her sari—at the moment, she was one with the image that her election campaigners had spun out for her: faultless to perfection. But her advisors travelling with her were filled with apprehensions.

'Artiji,' one of her campaigners looked at her, 'I think, you should not venture out in these areas without police bandobast.'

'You are scared?' Her smile spoke of too many things—of her faith in basic human nature, of her arrogance, her innocence of the ground realities, even of her naivete. And above all it failed to reassure her campaigners.

'No! I mean,' he chose his words carefully, 'It would be better. What if there is a riot ... or an agitated mob or something?'

'Who will riot against me?' she was awakening to the challenge. She took the sunglasses off her eyes.

'The public would not do anything against you ... but there are people who can manipulate others .. .make them do things ...' the threat was palpable in the air.

'There are stories doing the rounds that the opposition does not like your being here ... what if you ...'

'You do not worry about me ... the opposition is a decent honest lot ... they are not ruffians or goons.'

The election campaign was at its zenith. The tension between the rival campaigners was so thick that you could cut it with a knife. Arti Devi's cavalcade sped through the city. Though Arti Devi's supporters and campaigners had drummed up a massive cry for Arti Devi, one could still see small pickets of rival supporters, all through the route. And the closer Arti Devi came to the place where she was supposed to address the gathering of her supporters, the more fervid and feverish became the activities of the opposition. And finally, Arti Devi's cavalcade came to a crashing halt. The road in front of them was blockaded. No sooner had the car stopped that Lallu Lal sprang out of the car and held the door open for Arti Devi. Arti Devi stepped out of the car to assess the situation.

'Madam, This road is blocked and most likely, we will come across such blockades throughout.'

'Never mind, we will walk,' she was determined to go ahead, 'It is very important to attend the meeting.'

Arti Devi strode through the crowd. On her feet. Her supporters, though not visibly pleased with her audacity, had to follow suit.

A crowd invariably develops both an entity and identity of its own. And it feeds on its own anger. This crowd was going to be no exception. Somewhere, somehow the crowd turned belligerent—it did not tolerate Arti Devi's audacity to confront it, to try to walk through it and it showed its displeasure. A stone was pelted and then some more. Soon, it was free for all. A well-directed stone found Arti Devi. It cut through her forehead and then all mayhem broke lose.

Lallu Lal showing presence of mind, somehow commandeered a car and whisked Arti Devi to the safety of the hotel.

Gursaran, the old party faithful, came running to Lallu Lal, 'Send for a doctor ... quick!'

Lallu Lal looked at Gursaran as if he was a naïve fool, 'Bhaiye, let the press arrive first ... If you must call somebody, then call a photographer! Here, come here, bhaiye!' he beckoned a party worker, 'Aye, bhaiye, get the hotel staff to send for a doctor. Bhaiye, let the news spread! Now that there is fire ... fan it! Let it swell. What will you get if you try to put the fire out now ... just a room full of smoke ... the smoke will only burn your eyes and do nothing else for you ... understand ... let the fire smoulder.'

Amrit walked into JK's office. JK was engrossed in his files.

'Sir!'

'Yes!'

'Sir, Arti Devi has been injured! Chandersen pelted her with stones!'

'Chandersen?'

'Yes, I mean Chandersen has got it done ... through his partymen ... they pelted stones at her. She had gone to Kinnarpur to attend a meeting and the opposition party started throwing stones. I believe she is badly wounded.'

'Where is she now?'

'Upstairs, in her room.'

'Go and fetch Doctor Gokhale immediately,' he picked up the receiver to dial a number, hesitated and then replaced the receiver on the cradle.

'Yes, Sir.'

'Take my car.'

Once again, he began to dial a number but stopped. He kept staring at the telephone. The news had made him distraught, completely shaken him.

The news of the dastardly attack on Arti Devi soon spread like wildfire and reporters of every shade and hue, of every faith and belief began to pour into Hotel Aashiana.

JK walked out of his office and traversed the distance to the South Wing. He just could not control himself.

Outside Arti Devi's suite in the hotel, the old faithful

Gursaran was explaining to a party worker, 'Listen, there is a press conference going on inside. Don't let anyone enter.'

'Yes sir ... will do so.' He stood guard at the door.

No sooner had Gursaran issued these instructions and gone inside that JK walked in.

The party worker stopped JK.

'I want to meet Arti Devi.'

'Where have you come from?'

'I am the Manager of this hotel.'

The guard looked at JK. A manager—he could be safely dismissed, 'Come after some time. Right now she is busy with the press conference.'

'Only for a minute.'

'Please do not disturb.' He folded his hand telling JK in no uncertain terms that he was not willing to entertain him any further. JK could not do anything about it. He walked away.

This was a different Arti Devi who addressed a room full of press people. She walked with measured and assured steps. When she spoke, her words seared through the reporters ... her gaze bore into them ... she was not going to brook any assault on her.

'I see no reason why people would throw stones at me or, for that matter, at any other candidate? Why would they? They are not cowards. This is an act of cowardice. Only cowards behave in this fashion. Only cowards are scared of the rival's strength. They are cowards who don't have confidence in themselves. They are cowards who stoop this low. Only cowards resort to such dastardly acts. Why would the common man resort to pelting stones? The people have great power in their hands. Their greatest strength is in their hands! In their votes! They have the power to throw out anyone they do not like!'

Her head bandaged, she strode the room and everything she said, the press lapped up.

'Who do you think is behind this? Whose handiwork is this—Chandersen or Gul Sher Khan?'

'This is the work of hatred, of pettiness! Not of any one else.'

'Can't this hatred stem from the public?' A lone voice in the sea of reporters.

'If the public hated me, then one lakh people would not have gathered in this scorching heat, to attend that meeting! And they had to return disappointed after four hours of wait. If the public hates me, they don't need my permission to remove me. Don't underestimate the people. They know both work and responsibility. But those who resort to violence will have to learn the importance of work and responsibility. Those who have no faith left in democracy, they will have to learn. Those who want to get elected with violence, by throwing stones, they have a lot to learn.'

'Isn't violence a part of politics?' another pertinent question.

'Certainly, it is! Part of bad politics.' The press was eating out of her hands now.

'Tell us, why is the opposition so against you ?'

'They are against me, that is why they are in the opposition.'

The press got a taste of her burnished wit and it burst into peals of laughter. Nothing like laughter to resuscitate a tired gathering.

'They often ask what has the government done for the people ... can't they see it for themselves that the farmers of today are not serfs but their own landlords ... we make our own war planes to defend ourselves ... today, every village has a school, a hospital and electricity ... were there any before ... who has brought about these changes ... the government does not possess the lamp of Alladin—one rub and the problem is solved ... ask these leaders, ask them ...

just once ... how many of them file their tax returns honestly with the government ... and to top it all, they go on strike ... they exhort the police and the military to give up their duties and mutiny ...'

'They say all is fair in love and war?'

'Yes, absolutely correct! I would like to ask my brothers in the opposition just a simple question—are we fighting an election or a war? If it is a war then why are they using prehistoric weapons such as stones and catapults? Why don't they use rifles and revolvers? And if it is not a war, but love, then please convey my gratitude to them for this token of love.' And she pointed her fingers at her freshly bandaged head.

A bubble of laughter rippled through the room.

And as if on cue, Lallu Lal made a dramatic entry with the doctor. 'Deviji, please don't strain yourself,' he said showing much concern, 'I have brought the doctor sahib with me. Please get your wound dressed by him.'

By now, Arti Devi had become the darling of the masses. She came into her element in front of them. And she knew that. And her campaigners knew that too.

Arti Devi got up to leave.

She moved towards the door of her room when a reporter followed her for one final question.

'Excuse me, Ma'am ... one last question, please ...'

'Yes?'

'This accident ... that has happened ... whom would you hold responsible for this?'

'Certainly you cannot fault destiny,' she tried to explain, 'Nor can you fault the poor stones lying lifelessly on the road that suddenly found life of their own and began to rain on my head! Obviously, some hands must have moved towards them to pick them ... some hands must have been raised to hurl them but ... but, it is not for me to stop those hands or to saw them off ...' A silence fell on the gathering and she let that silence speak for her, to fill in the details. A silence that would wreak more havoc than any word could. And when the silence had done its work, she slowly found her voice back, '... that is the job of the public!'

Chandersen threw the newspaper on the table. A bandaged Arti Devi hogged the entire front page of the *Watan.* Arti Devi, his anathema, screaming from the front page—it was too much for Chandersen to stomach. He repeatedly pointed to the paper, chastising his supporters for making it come to pass.

'Have you read this? Have you?? Arti Devi blames the opposition! My foot!'

His rage was inconsolable, 'As if we are the ones who threw stones at her! Just look at her audacity! And that Gyani he had to print this on the front page!'

'I think you should also call a press conference and clarify your position,' it was an innocent suggestion from Kartar. Chandersen turned about to face him. The silver in his hair caught the light and glinted, 'Beg your pardon? What did you just say? Call a press conference, should I?'

'Yes, Sir,' Kartar stood by his initial suggestion.

'To give a clarification?'

'Yes...yes, Sir.'

Chandersen looked at Kartar as if he was looking not at the veteran of numerous elections campaigns but at a recent initiate, 'You mean if the axe hasn't fallen on my foot, I should put my foot on the axe! Is that what you want?'

'But the people think that it is we who initiated the riots ...'

Chandersen did not give him the chance to finish what he was saying. He pounced on him. 'This is exactly what she wants to prove to the people—prove that she is the only peace-loving leader ... as if the rest of us are gangsters, hoodlums, boors who do not understand democracy, ruffians who cannot function in a democracy.'

'But how did this riot happen?' Kartar was now making an effort to divert the heat.

'People must have started on their own free will.' Another supporter took the probe.

Chandersen arched his eyebrows as if he was being humoured by a court of fools, 'Now look here, one thing is certain—nothing happens here of its own free will ... people do not react unless and until provoked.'

'And since we did not provoke them, that means Gul Sher Khan did!' they were finally seeing things Chandersen's way.

'Who else? This is what happens when such rank amateurs enter politics. They play the tune and we have to face the music!' His eyes once again caught Arti Devi's picture on the front page and he clenched his teeth, 'this Gyani ...' he pounded the newspaper, 'he needs to answer me ... how dare he let her hog the entire front page ... how dare he ?'

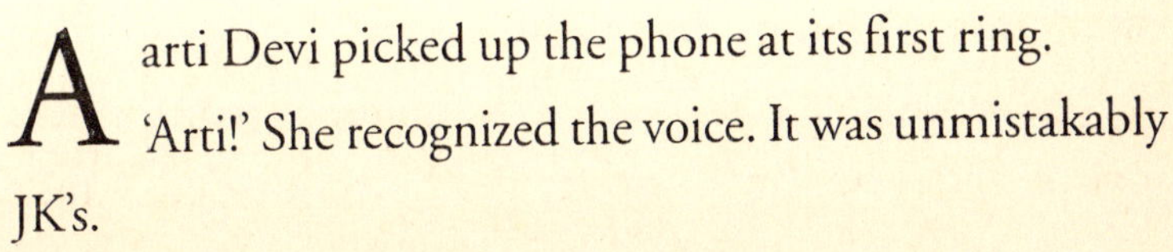

Arti Devi picked up the phone at its first ring.

'Arti!' She recognized the voice. It was unmistakably JK's.

'Please hold on for a moment,' she cupped her hand over the black bakelite of the telephone mouthpiece and looked at Lallu Lal. He was ensconced comfortably in the spotless white divan.

'Why don't you fix the program with Gursaranji. You will find him in the office downstairs. He can let me know later.'

'Very well, namaste,' Lallu Lal got up and left.

Arti Devi relaxed a little, reclined against the bolster,

'Hello!'

JK was right down the line, 'You were impossible to meet yesterday ... I tried very hard.'

'Yes. Too many visitors.'

'How are you feeling now?'

'Nothing to worry,' she tapped the taped wound on her temple, 'just a minor bruise. Even the scar will be gone before the night falls.'

'But the papers tell a different story,' his concern was not mitigated by her response.

'Don't you believe everything that is printed in the papers. The whole thing has just got blown out of proportion. You know very well ... why ...' She did not have to take recourse to the devious dynamics of politics with him.

'Yes, I can hazard a guess.' Relief crept into his words.

'I learnt from Gursaranji that you had come yesterday. Choudhry sahib didn't let you in. He doesn't know you. Gursaranji does.'

'Ah...ha ... come over for lunch this afternoon ... Binda is cooking saag for you. You are still fond of it, aren't you?'

'I won't be here this afternoon, but ask him to save some for me.' A pause. 'May I have dinner with you tonight?'

'Yes, yes of course! Why not? You'll come over ... home?'

'Aa haan ...' Home was what she had been so far away from. And home was what was near at hand. She controlled the quiver in her voice but tears began to betray her feelings. JK was not around to see them, so she let them flow. 'Tell Binda Kaka that as long as I am here, I will have dinner at home every night.' Tears have a way of flowing both inwards and outwards. JK couldn't see the tears that flowed so copiously down her cheeks, but what about those that had begun to flow inwards and had started to choke her voice. JK could hear those tears and she did not want him to. She abruptly replaced the receiver in the cradle. JK could only hear a distant click, the suddenness of which he was unable to fathom.

That evening Arti Devi hosted a dinner for the prominent denizens of the city on the lawns of Hotel Aashiana. As the manager of the hotel, JK oversaw everything. He left no room for any complaints: the menu was exotic; the wines were of a good vintage; the cigars were authentic, Cuban. JK strolled around, nodding his head in greeting. He was well turned out in a silver grey lounge suit. He stopped where Arti Devi sat under the glow of twin candles in an antique candelabra. He was seeing her for the first time since the stone-pelting incident.

'Hello Ma'am ... How are you?'

'Fine, thank you.'

'How is the head? I mean the injury on the head?'

'Don't worry ... see ...' she pointed to the wound on her temple.

JK bent down to take a closer look, and accidentally touched the wound. She winced in pain.

' Oh ... oh ... I am sorry. You got hurt on the temple?'

'No, actually the stone stuck me on the head ... nothing to get worked up about.'

'Still, you shouldn't have gone to such a place.'

'I had to . . .that's what I do!'

'Yes, I know.' He looked at her and finding her alone for

the moment, ventured to ask 'Coming home at night for dinner, aren't you?'

'Yes, and if I am free early, I will cook.'

'Really?' he could not believe his ears. 'So you still know how to cook?'

'What do you think?'

'Well I shall reserve my opinion for after the act!'

She would come home to cook. To cook. Did he hear her correctly, did he? He turned to go. And as he moved away, he knocked against a glass.

'Sorry, my fault, I shouldn't have put the glass there.' She was profusely apologetic.

JK bent down to pick the glass up and he inspected the contents.

'Nimbu-paani !!' he looked amused, 'since when did you switch to nimbu-paani?'

'How do you mean?'

A hint of mischief sneaked into his eyes, 'Shall I send over a cola for you?'

'Cola? What cola?' she could not bridge the reference with the past, not yet.

'Why, the kind you were drunk on that evening when we first met.'

'You still remember it?'

'Does one forget a first meeting? Ever??' He leaned against the arm of her chair, a glass in one hand and a faraway look in his eyes.

Resplendent in an azure blue sari with pearl-white flowers embroidered on them, two strands of pearls offsetting the jet black curls dangling against her kohl-lined eyes, Arti Devi strode into the hotel lobby and walked towards the front-office, albeit a bit unsteadily. JK looked up from his books at her. When she spoke, she slurred.

'Can I ... gait a. a. loom here?'

JK looked up at her. She was clearly inebriated. He picked up the hotel register and put it in front of her, 'Would you like to have a single room or a double room?'

'I want a room!' Like a pampered rich girl used to ordering people around, she banged the desk and spoke incoherently, 'Give me ...' She raised her hands to bang again but JK caught her hands midway, 'Room? You want a room? Fine, but must you break your hands over it?'

He moved from the desk to get the room-key. A whisper, 'JK, do you know who she is?'

JK looked at his desk clerk. 'No. Who is she?'

'Arti, K Bose's daughter.'

JK looked at her again with renewed interest, trying to picture the connection of this at-the-moment-in-a-not-so-honorable-condition daughter and the very honourable mayor. At this moment, it was clearly a struggle for her to even stay steady... even stay put on her feett. 'The Mayor's daughter? K. Bose's daughter? How do you know?'

'Hu'n ... I have seen her with him in the meetings... at functions ... many a times, at many an occasion.'

Arti Devi could not even walk out of the hotel lift on her own. She stumbled and would have hit the floor had not JK stepped forward to give her support. She was, however, making desperate efforts to stay coherent, to make sense of herself, but she was certainly not succeeding. JK led her towards the room while she kept on her patter.

'They ... they played a prank on me. How can I go home like this ...?' A patch of silence and then, 'Wh... where ... is ... the... car ...?'

'Car ... whose car?'

'My Fiat?'

'It must be downstairs. Come, be careful!'

'Bring it up!'

'The car? Here?'

'Yes!'

'Upstairs!!'

'Yes!'

'How?'

'Bring it on a tray ...'

JK burst out laughing.

'That's common sense ... use some common sense!' she slurred on.

Somehow containing himself, JK fumbled with the key, 'Ah…now that never occurred to me!'

He opened the door and ushered Arti Devi into the room.

JK walked back to the desk clerk, back to business, 'Get the AC fixed in 302.'

'Sure,' but the desk clerk was more solicitous of the mayor's inebriated daughter, 'So which room have you put Mr. Bose's daughter in?'

'212.'

'Don't you think we should let Mr. Bose know about this.'

'Forget it man ... why get the poor thing into trouble.'

'What if Mr. Bose gets to know about it later on? They are important people, you know.'

'I don't give a damn as to who they are! For us, customers are esteemed guests and that's all!' JK dismissed the matter.

Just about then, a waiter rushed in. He looked panicky.

'Sir...sir ... that room 212 ... that room ...'

'Yes ... what's it with 212?'

'The water sir ... it ... it is gushing out from under the door. I rang the bell. . .kept on ringing it, but ... but ... there's no response Sir!'

JK stepped out from behind the desk. The desk clerk did not want to be left out of the action, especially when it concerned the Mayor's daughter, 'Shall I come along too?'

'Don't worry ... I shall take care of it!' he turned, 'find out if there's any Fiat parked outside with a flat tire.'

And JK rushed towards the lift.

JK rang the doorbell again and again. Then pressed on it non-stop. But the door remained shut. JK forced the door open with his master key and stepped gingerly into the room. The room was in utter disarray and Arti Devi was nowhere to be seen. A stream of water streaked the carpet. He could hear the shower running. He followed the spate of water into the bathroom. All the shower and taps were running. Only her legs were visible. The rest of Arti Devi lay submerged in the brimming tub. JK was amused. He began to turn the taps off one by one. Her striking azure blue sari was half-strewn across the floor, still half wrapped around her.

The next morning, JK had Arti's azure blue sari laundered and pressed. With it neatly draped on a wooden hanger, he wended his way to room 212. Every time his eyes fell on the sari, he could not help giving an amused smile. He stood outside her hotel room door and pressed the call button. The bell resonated inside the room where Arti Devi must have only stirred awake a few minutes earlier. Finding herself on a strange bed, with a comforter wrapped around her, she was trying to make sense out of it all.

'Come in!'

JK strode into the room, ' Good Morning!'

Arti Devi was not expecting a man. This only confounded her further.

JK strode towards the wardrobe and hung her sari inside. 'Had to take your clothes away.'

Arti Devi fought back the images the words suggested and hugged the comforter tighter. 'Who took them off?' she finally mustered some courage to ask. It was hardly audible.

'Yes? Did you say something?'

'Who removed these clothes?' A little louder this time.

'From where? You didn't ask that!' he picked up the upturned table lamp. 'How come you are not asking me how you reached here? Who brought you here ... from where?' He picked up the bulb that had come unhinged. He held it against the light to see if the filament had snapped with the fall.

Arti looked so vulnerable. 'Where ... from where?'

'From the bathroom, in this condition ... the condition in which you are now?'

She had feared the worst. And the worst had come to pass. 'Oh, no!'

'Oh yes ... that's the truth. I guess you had one-too many to drink last evening. And in that drunken stupor you marched across my lobby, to my desk and demanded a room. That was duly given to you. And after getting in here, I guess you wanted to scrub your intoxication away and walked straight into the bathroom ... and then ... must you ask me what happened?'

She was horrified at the possibilities. She kept looking at him, wide-eyed.

'When I found you ... the taps were running ... and you ... you were knocked off ... absolutely blacked out ...'

Arti was too embarrassed to even look up at him.

'And then a clerk recognized you ... told me whose daughter you are ... So I ...' he looked at her ... her face had suddenly turned ashen, 'so I did not let your father know.'

Arti felt she could breathe again.

'I thought it may not be good for you ... now please change your clothes ... no ... I mean wear your clothes. Next time around ... carry a change of clothes in your car.'

'I am sorry. It ... it's not a habit with me ... last evening ... somebody pulled a prank on me ... somebody laced my cola

with liquor ... I did not realize it ... and in the course of the evening had about four ... maybe ... five ... drinks ... and then it suddenly hit me ... I must have been too drunk when I left the place. But it was in the car that I realized that I was in no state to go home. I didn't know where to go. I just wanted to bury my face some place. I remember parking the car ...'

JK chuckled, 'You call that parking your car?'

'How do you mean?'

'A wheel on the sidewalk, another into the flower pot ... and of the two that stayed on the road ... one was punctured.'

'Oh, no!'

'Oh yes!'

'Huh!!'

'Anyway, I have got your car fixed...have a look at it when you come down.'

JK escorted Arti Devi to her car and held the door open. 'Here's your car and that's what remains of our flower pot ... poor thing!'

Arti Devi looked at the smashed flowerpot – she lowered her head, all the while curling the ends of a lock of her hair around her fingers in nervous agitation, only managing an embarrassed smile. 'I am sorry.'

JK brushed the apology aside, 'And here's your car key!'

'I am very grateful to you.'

'You're welcome ... but don't you worry ... I shall have the bill sent across.'

'Oh ... I ...' she dug in her purse but she realized that there was no money in it. Her face turned crimson.

'Never mind,' JK tried to make light of it, 'You can send the money later, but next time, you must carry some money with you. You never know when the need arises ... in times such as these ....'

'This will never happen ... ever again!'

A smile spread across JK's face, ear to ear. And that bothered her.

'Really, I mean it,' she was more emphatic this time.

'Promise?' he extended his hand.

Arti Devi looked at the proffered hand, hesitated, looked at him and then in an impulse put hers in his. 'Promise!' The next instant, she turned away and climbed into the car, a coy smile stealing into her face.

She turned the ignition on. The car purred to life. She let the engine idle and took out a visiting card and gave it to JK. 'This is my address. Come over some time,' it sounded pretty formal, so she added a personal note, 'Please do come. I will wait for you.' And she put the car in gear. The car lurched forward.

JK looked after the car with amusement. A whistle escaped

his lips. A breeze ruffled his hair. He quietly tore the card, twice over and tossed it in the breeze. Hardly had he taken a few steps that Arti Devi reversed the car and caught up with him.

'I am sorry. I think I gave you the wrong card. May I have that one back please?'

'Card? Oh, yes ... JK was caught unawares. He pretended to look for it in his pocket. Arti pulled out another card and handed it over to him, 'Before you tear up this one, wait for me to pull out of your hotel ... I can catch you in the rear view mirror.' The table had been neatly turned—it was JK's turn to be embarrassed, and he was.

Fate brought them together again. Outside a bookshop. Their chance acquaintanceship was renewed. They found themselves gravitating towards one another. And their friendship grew over shared cups of coffee, shared books and a love for poetry. She loved the way he wrote. He loved the way she responded to his written words. Whenever he penned down a new idea, a new poem he knew no peace till he had read it out to her. It was one of those nights. He had just finished composing a new poem. The ink had not yet dried on the paper. The pen was still in his hand uncapped and the phone cradled in the crook of his neck. Arti was on the other side of the night, in her room. He spoke slowly into the phone, feeling the weight of every word on his lips. She picked up the phone and traversed the entire length of her bedroom and sat on the edge of her bed, her ear glued onto the phone.

Aao tumko uthaa lu'n kandhon par
Tum uchak kar sharir hothon se
Choom lena yeh chand ka maatha
Aaj ki raat dekhna tum bhi
Kaise jhuk-jkuk ke kohniyon ke bal
Chand itna kareeb aaya hai ...!!

Come let me prop you on my shoulders
and you strain on your toes
to kiss with your impish lips
the forehead of the moon
Come be witness to this night
how the moon has crawled on his elbows
Just to be near you

Arti Devi was simply bowled over by his imagery. 'Beautiful! Wonderful!'

'It's good, isn't it?

'It is.'

'When you say it's good, it feels really good.'

Arti's eyes lit up with an impish glee, 'You know if your poems were not a part of you ... you would have been a very ordinary man.'

'But it was meant to be! You see I was just twelve when I began to get invited to mushairas.'

'You achieved every single feat when you were twelve.' She was in the mood for banter.

'Yes everything, except getting married.' They picked up the old thread of conversation a couple of days later.

Arti chuckled, 'And pray tell me what stopped you from achieving that feat too.'

'Had I met you then, I would have done that too.'

'Thank me ... I saved you from a life of bachelorhood!' And she stole a look at him and moved away. He followed her.

Aarti Devi's desire to marry JK hunched the shoulders of Bose a little. He took the Meerschaum out of his mouth, measured a few steps towards the unlit fireplace of his study. The patch of baldness glinted against his spotless white kurta pyjama and the expensive shawl drooped against his shoulders. He looked at candelabra on the mantelpiece, 'You want to get married?' Arti Devi's announcement had devastated him. He turned. Arti Devi stood against the bookshelf, her eyes downcast, her fingers wrapped around the strands of pearls around her neck. 'Why ...? What is the hurry? What will you achieve by getting married? Tell me ... tell me ... explain to me?'

His gaze bore into Arti Devi, desperately trying to decipher where he had gone wrong. Arti Devi did not lift her eyes. Her Oxford education had not taken away her Indianness, albeit it had only given her the concession to raise the subject of her own marriage with her father. She did not lift her eyes to meet his. The father was expecting an answer but none was forthcoming.

'As far as I know ...' he came near her ... looked at her ... she could not lift her eyes to his ... she began to scribble something with her pencil on the buff file that she was holding.

'... at least thirty-eight thousand marriages take place every day in our country. Out of which one marriage will be yours. What next? What about your future?'

She could not deny that there was a certain cold logic in her father's arguments. But she was her father's daughter after all: she would not be cowed down that easily. Her gaze was downcast, but there was defiance in her stance. She shifted her gaze from the file to the tip of her pencil.

The father dragged on his Meerschaum—the pipe had since grown cold and he moved away from her. A few measured steps and he was once again in the distant corner of the room—the daughter's defiance translated in the physical distance. 'The cleaning woman who comes to our house has also got married. Within a few years of marriage she has been saddled with children ... you too will have children, but then ... then what?' he reached the end of the room ... and it was then that he noticed that the fire had gone out of his Meerschaum, but he let it be. He turned towards his daughter, 'Is this what you want out of life? To reduce it to this? Is this going to be the goal of your life, then? Is this your ambition?' his voice peaked a little. But she was his daughter, his only child. His tone softened but the heartbreak tinted his voice, 'I am very disappointed, my dear. You just want to be one of the millions and millions of ...' He looked despairingly at his daughter ... no ... she could not be just one of them—'those creatures.' He took one step towards her, his gaze boring through her, in the hope that she might see some sense. Arti Devi's face stayed calm but her defiance and unhappiness at her father's expostulation manifested itself in the way she played the strands of pearls with her pencil in agitation.

The father tried to stoke her dormant ambitions, 'I had so many hopes for you ... I wanted to see you at great heights ... but now in your haste to get married ...'

'No, no. I am in no great hurry to get married,' JK stood up from his wicker chair and moved away from her, 'It's okay with me. I have waited so many years, I can wait some more, but what about you?'

She too got up, moved towards him, looked at him and then at the palms of her hand. 'But I can't!'

'Then? Then what are we to do?'

'We will get married,' she looked at him and blushed. But her determination was unshakeable.

'And what is to become of your politicking?'

'That you will need to do!'

'And what will you do?' he laughed at the very thought of it.

'I have fallen in your lot. I will chop onions in the kitchen,' she wiped imaginary tears from her eyes.

'And what else?' he was amused.

'I will bore you ...'

'That is obvious ... and what else?'

'I will make your life miserable.'

'And?'

'Okay, baba!!,' she reached out for his shirt, the top button had come undone and she buttoned it, 'I'll do everything ... stitch clothes ... knead dough... fry dal... okay?'

'If this was all that you wanted to do then what was the need to waste five years at Oxford?' Mr Bose buttoned his

waistcoat, straightened his necktie and moved towards the dressing table to pick up his cufflinks. A picture of the handsome Nehru hung over the wall: Nehru in deep conversation with his beautiful daughter Indira. Many a times Bose saw a reflection of the father-daughter duo in himself and his daughter. Now, this reflection was being threatened by her base desire to get married. He sighed and pointed to the photograph, 'Do you know the kind of sacrifices this girl had to make?? If big ambitions are to be achieved you have to forego these trivial pleasures!'

Arti Devi looked at the picture, 'It is she who has always been my ideal,' her voice was emotionally strained, 'Daddy, I may not become her ... but I can at least try to follow her example.'

The father picked up his coat and hung it on his hand, 'I want you to join politics! Attain a position in life... let my business too benefit from it.'

In one single statement, the father shattered all perceptions of the daughter, this was not what she had expected from her father. She was expecting high ideals, but she would not be held hostage to the profiteering need of a shrewd businessman, even if that businessman happened to be her father.

But oblivious to the emotions his words had evoked, Mr Bose carried on, 'You don't understand anything, do you? If you progress in life, so will my business ... these days without politics ...'

That was enough. Arti Devi could not take his spiel any longer. 'Don't make my life your business daddy! I wanted to join politics to serve my country ... not to run shop for you! And I am quitting it to start a family of my own.'

And she stormed out of the room.

Memories are treacherous little things. They sit in some unseen corners of the mind to clutch at the heart at unpredictable moments. The passage of time had greyed his hair but it refused to dull his memories. Memories throbbed and synchronized their beats with the dull tom-tom of his heart. 'I was just thinking,' he stole a look at her—how gorgeous she looked with the pallu of her sari over her head, 'You said you would cook when you came home,' he took his hands off his pockets and looked at his watch, 'but Binda must have finished cooking by now.'

'I got late ... getting out ...' there was an apology in her smile.

'Never mind. So, when did you cook last time?'

'When I was twelve years old ...'

He stopped abruptly to look at her. She had misappropriated his turn of phrase. A silence engulfed them for a moment and then their laughter filled the silence, and all those years that had kept them apart.

Arti, with her saree tucked in, was frying dal in the kitchen. She stepped back with a start to avoid the fumes.

Binda laughed, 'What are you doing, beti? Here, give it to me. This is my job. Now you are doing great work ... solving the country's problems ... why are you getting into this? Leave this dal-val business to me? You must be out of practice by now, having left it long years ago ...'

'So much has been left behind, long ago ... everything, Kaka, my home... my people ... everything got left behind ...'

'Why do you say this? Relationships don't wither away if you don't meet! What good is a relationship that crumbles when you let go of the hand? Go and call sahib for dinner. I will get the table ready by then.'

Arti moved towards the dining room. On the verge of calling out to him, she hesitated. An Indian woman never addresses her husband by his name. Was she modern enough to do away with the shackles of tradition. She debated the issue. Binda turned to find her still in the kitchen. 'You still here ... Go and call him! What are thinking about?'

'How should I address him?' the eloquent Arti Devi knew how to address a gathering of lakhs but did not know how to address her husband.

'What?'

'How do you address him?'

'I call him sahib. But you won't call him by that name,' he laughed.

'Okay, how do people address him?'

'They call him JK sahib. But you are not people! Okay, I'll call him.'

'No! You think I can't call him! I will go. I will call him.' But the question remained unanswered. She was meeting him after so many years that she wasn't sure what was left between them. How should she address him?

JK sat in his drawing room, leafing through the pages of an old photo-album. Arti Devi walked in and looked at him and she simply chose to dispense with the entire question and settled for, 'Dinner is served!'

He kept the album aside and began to get up.

Arti Devi looked at the album, came and picked it up,

'What were you looking at?'

'An old album.'

She came and sat at the edge of the diwan and turned a leaf. Their daughter stared back at her, 'Here ... Mannu looks a bit plump?'

'She has taken after her father.'

Arti Devi looked at JK and smiled and then turned another leaf in the album, 'When was this taken?'

'Last year. There are some ruins nearby. A favorite haunt of Mannu's.'

'Looks great.'

'It is. I can show you around, if you wish.'

'How can I!' She barely managed to chisel out some time with JK from her ever-demanding schedule.

'If not by day, then come in the night.'

'When?'

'Why, tonight? After dinner?'

'You will show me around?'

'Yes.'

'Promise?'

'Promise!'

Moonlight filtered through the broken colonnades of the ruins, strangely illuminating the darkness—here, a brightness of artistic excellence; there, a shadow of untold cruelties that the centuries of invaders had inflicted on its grandeur. It must have been majestic once, now reduced to mere relics of a different time, of a bygone era, and yet so pleasing to the eye. Arti Devi and JK walked out of the darkness of the archways, into the light of the moon. Their relationship too was in a way a relic of a different time.

Arti Devi looked around. She nearly lost her balance on the loose stones of the ruins. JK took her hand in his, lending her support, The face of the ruins felt familiar, 'I have come out after years, it seems.'

JK looked at her, 'Years, yes ... these monuments must have been in their prime the last time you were here!'

A sadness tinged her voice, 'Yes, they must have been ... it does feel so ... a lifetime ago ... maybe in a previous birth.'

JK pulled her off the pebbly path, 'As long as you are here, you are dining at home, why don't we steal a few hours every night and come here ... at least for a few days these desolated monuments will find their happiness resurrected.'

His words scrounged her for an answer. Arti Devi looked

away from him, into the night. The helpless night stared back at her with its bottomless darkness deepened further by the bursts of moonlight. The night had suddenly begun to feel cold, she pulled the pallu of her sari around her.

'Where's your shawl?'

'I ... I ... I,' she began to tug at the edge of her pallu, 'I ... I ... forgot it at home.' By now, JK had taken off his coat and in spite of her protests wrapped it around her shoulders, 'You will never change.'

She slowly raised her gaze to find his. And they moved along the ruins. They had moved along in life as well and done well for themselves, even without each other. But the moment they looked at each other they knew that they may have carried on with their lives, but they had not lived life. They *were* each other's life. They knew this, but neither was willing to admit this to the other. The shadows of the ruins lengthened and engulfed them. They traversed that tunnel of darkness and emerged into the light once again. They sat on the steps of the ruins, lit by the moon—their lives, a cumulative sigh, like the darkness behind them. The moon streaked her hair silver. But a few moments of togetherness can never be an apologia for the years spent apart. The magic was only for the moment. They got up, moved ahead. An entire ruin lay ahead. They stopped in front of the baroque of another wall. 'Look, Arti, look at them! These creepers that you see, are not really creepers. They are aayats engraved in Arabic! If you come here during the day, you can see them clearly ... during the day, this reservoir is full of water ... and these fountains ...'

'During the day,' if only she could, she would have invented a million reasons just to be with him, but she knew that would not be possible, 'Impossible for me to find the time during the day.' She was a prisoner of her own life and lived according to its dictate.

JK smiled and pointed at the pearly white globule of brightness in the sky, 'Well then, it leaves us with this moon ... it only comes out at night.'

And they both chuckled at their own helplessness.

'Well, it must be coming out every day.'

'Yes that's there ... but in between, there are nights of absolute darkness ... moonless nights. Usually, there are only fifteen nights without the moon ... but this time the darkness stretched itself a bit too long.'

'Nine years long...wasn't it?' She looked up at him. He found her eyes flooded with pain, awash with tears. She tried to move away from him but couldn't. And she clung onto his arms. And she wished that she could bury herself forever, for all times to come, in his arms. But that was not meant to be. Her tears hid her emotional betrayal within themselves.

Lallu Lal walked with measured steps towards his chair and sunk himself in it. On the wall behind him was nailed a huge image of Arti Devi and her election symbol. Lallu Lal looked at the party worker, 'There is one way to break Chandrasen, and that is to make Aggarwal file his candidacy in this election.'

'What will we gain out of it?'

Lallu Lal looked at the man as if he had just walked in from a god-forsaken place, he crossed his hands over the desk, tilted his head confidently, 'Bhaiyye ... first tell me ... how many votes would you need to win if the opposition has ten votes?'

'Eleven.'

Lallu Lal reclined against the chair, 'And suppose, I split these ten votes in two groups of five each, then how many votes would you need?'

'Six!'

'There you are!'

'Now that's a good idea, but you know Arti Devi . . what if she gets to know about it?'

'Bhaiyye!! That's the reason why I am telling you this. . .so that she does not get wind about it. . .you keep your mouth zipped and your eyes shut!'

'But how are you going to pull off this stunt?'

Lallu Lal sat across the table with the bottle of his medicine between him and Aggrawal. 'Now you tell me, Aggrawal Sahib, if I contest the elections, who will my children vote for? They'll vote for me, obviously.'

'Yes, of course,' Aggrawal reclined against his plush leather chair. His office screamed opulence, and so did the strands of precious gemstones that he wore outside his expensive hand-stitched silk jacket.

'And you are the mai-baap of the workers.'

'Yes, that's true,' Aggrawal was easy to flatter.

'They won't even have to think about Chandersen and Arti Devi. They don't care about them. All their votes are already in your pocket,' Lallu Lal knew how to pander to vain people.

'That is true,' he fell for it, hook line and sinker.

'And you have the business class voters in your other pocket.'

'They are my community.'

'Aggrawal sahib, it is very clear ... you are the one who sways the balance ... wherever you go ... that party will win

... it's you who make parties wins. Whoever you support, is going to win,' he picked up his 'medicine' bottle, ready for the celebration, 'then, why don't you contest the elections yourself?'

'I never thought of that,' new vistas were opening up before Aggarwal.

'Oh, you don't have to think, Aggrawal Sahib. Leave the thinking to the likes of me.'

Aggarwal was in. He lit his cigarette. He had taken the plunge. It was time for celebration. Lallu Lal uncorked his bottle of 'medicine' and took a big swig.

'What is this medicine for?'

'It's for my kidneys. If I don't take it, my kidneys don't function properly.' Aggarwal was easier than he thought he would be. The 'medicine' refreshed him and he put forth his agenda, 'So Aggarwal sahib, I was saying ... not only are you giving votes to Chandersen but also your money. Am I right?'

'Right.'

'You must have given him at least a lakh and a half by now?' Lallu Lal had done his homework. He knew his facts and knew that he had to quote much below the amount Aggarwal had contributed to Chandersen's election funds.

'No, Sir,' he was chagrined, 'much more than that ... much more.'

'Bhaiye,' Lallu Lal knew his trick was turning, 'if he wins, his ten will turn into twenty ...'

'That's true!'

'And if he doesn't win ... then ...?'

'Then?'

'Arre, bhaiye ... you are in business. What have you got to do with his victory or defeat?' Lallu Lal drove the final nail in the coffin, 'Your money should not sink ... that's all?'

'That's true.'

'And if you invest the same money on yourself? Then you have no fear of losing it and no anxiety for gaining more. Aggrawal Sahib ... for you ... it's a win-win situation either way ... there is no chance of losing.'

'You have a point there,' Aggrawal was a lesson to be learnt in Lallu Lal's electioneering ways. He was totally and speedily brainwashed, 'There is substance in your argument.'

'Then what, bhaiye ... if you go by that, I will advise you to file your nomination papers at once!!'

Aggrawal stood up determinedly. Chandersen would soon find his election plans going haywire.

Chandersen was crestfallen. Lallu Lal's strategy had not only robbed him of his biggest fund contributor but also eroded his potential vote bank. He was worried sick, he paced the floor of his election office, 'Idiot! He is mad! He has gone insane! But what I can't understand is, who put this crazy idea in his head?'

'Who else but Lallu Lal,' Aggarwal's election symbol, the 'medicine' bottle made the conjecture easy, 'It has to be Lallu Lal. This 'medicine' bottle is his trademark. It has to be his idea.'

'Why would he do this? They can persuade him to join them then why would they want him to contest against them?' Chandersen still could not see sense in the logic.

'If Aggrawal contests, then what becomes of the workers' votes?'

'Obviously, he will get their votes. They are his mill-workers, after all.'

'But there is a massive strike going on in his mills since yesterday!' A party worker came in with the news.

'Strike? Why?' Both Chandersen and Choudhry were surprised to hear that.

'They have some demands.'

'Okay!' Finally an opportunity to strike, a hope streaked his eyes, 'Now, if his workers go against him, then what becomes of Aggrawal's strength? Avtar, instigate the workers. Don't let them come to any settlement ... at any cost.' Chandersen was jubilant.

A crowd of workers downed the shutters of Aggarwal's mills. They collected outside the mill gates, waving the red union flags. The crowd grew listless as the sun came overheard. But their sloganeering was uninterrupted. They kept up their chorus of their demands. The air was rent with their slogans: *Hamaari maangein poori karo ...*

We want our rights ...

Give us our rights ...

Aggrawal murdabad! Aggrawal murdabad!

And behind the crowd of mutineers, behind the red flags and the black placards of unfulfilled demands and unmitigated injustices stood Lallu Lal, reclining against the body of his jeep. A smile stretched his lips. He uncorked his medicine bottle and took a swig. He turned and climbed into his jeep and drove away.

Every action has a little price tag attached to it. And the night spent amongst the ruins with JK was to extract a huge price from Arti Devi. It was about to ruin everything. Only Arti Devi did not know it, not yet. She was under the spell of a terrible cold. She sneezed as she stepped out of the hotel lobby. She sneezed as she was stepping into her car.

Lallu Lal jumped out of the jeep as it came meandering into the hotel courtyard and he rushed towards Arti Devi, 'Everything is fine... all is going as planned. Now, first we will proceed to the Mahila Mandal, the women's organization ...'

It was then that JK came out and gave her a muffler and a bottle of medicine, 'Arti listen, take this. Take at least three doses of this medicine during the day. You have a bad cold'. Gursaran and Lallu Lal looked at each other in dismay, wondering at this sudden concern of the hotel manager.

JK noticed the prying eyes, the unvoiced questions, 'Last night I noticed that she had caught a severe cold. Here, keep this.'

Arti Devi suddenly looked sheepish as she took the medicine from him and stepped into her car. Lallu Lal interpreted this as a sign of guilt. His eyebrows arched as he saw Arti Devi's car move away. He moved towards his jeep, filled with foreboding.

'Bhaiye ... do you see what I see?' Lallu Lal loked at the driver of his jeep.

'What ... Sahib?' The driver looked surprised.

'The signs ... they do not augur well ... the weather's about to change.'

'Will it rain?' the driver, simpleton that he was, did not get his drift.

'Arre ... not just rain,' Lallu Lal was an experienced hand, 'It's going to thunder. A violent storm's brewing ... a thunderstorm! If the opposition party gets wind of it ... or even the slightest suspicion ... they will kick up a rumpus ... they'll make life miserable ...'

Lallu Lal's words were to soon prove prophetic. A photojournalist strode into Chandersen's newspaper office with an air of importance. He simply walked into his inner office and tossed a manila envelope in front of Chandersen.

'What's this?' Chandersen was curious.

'A few photographs, sir.'

Chandersen took out the photographs and as his eyes fell on them, his face lit up with hope. In black and white images lay revealed the story of the night JK and Arti Devi had spent amongst the ruins.

'Very Good! This is a great job you've done!' Chandersen saw his election victory close at hand.

'I had told you,' the reporter took pride in a job well done, 'I saw her in the Manager's house the other day ... and last night they were wandering among the ruins.'

'People may not have believed you. But who can deny these pictures? They will have to admit ... there is nothing left to imagination.'

'Here, take this, Avtar,' Chandersen handed the photographs to his executive editor, 'Now you have explosive material for *Zamana*. Go ahead and launch your paper with this news. Now, the line is all clear for us. Aggrawal will burn in the strike ... and this woman in the hotel ...'

Zamana could not have asked for a more sensational launch. ARTI DEVI'S NIGHT WITH HOTEL MANAGER screamed the headlines of the inaugural issue. And the photographs of Arti Devi with her hand in JK's filled the front page. It was a revelation for everybody. Arti Devi's campaign workers were shell-shocked.

Lallu Lal held his head in both his hands, 'We are ruined!' his voice was shrouded in mourning, 'What has this woman done?'

'All this is the mischief of Chandersen,' the party worker could not believe the slight of his leader.

'Arre, what mischief, bhaiye,' Lallu Lal saw all his hard work being flushed down the drain, ' Chandersen can be a liar, but this picture is not a lie! She won't be able show her face to anyone after this! She can't stand in public! This election is doomed. It's over even before it began! You think the opposition will spare her now? You think the public will forgive her? No! I speak from experience, and I tell you that even if God comes down to help her, she cannot win this election. It's over and done with. The end! You don't know the people!'

'What does anyone have to do with her private life anyway?' Party loyalists are hard to dissuade.

Lallu Lal turned to look at him, irritated with his naiveté, 'Bhaiyye, you don't win battles with the *Gita* in your hands ... Lord Krishna could not fight the battle, how will she?

'You don't understand, Lallu Lalji,' the party faithful was not to be deterred, 'this is where the opposition goofed up.'

Lallu Lal stares at him akimbo, 'How may that be?'

'A woman,' the man looked up from his work, 'can endure anything but a stain on her character.'

Arti Devi took off her tortoise-shell reading glasses off her eyes and walked into her election office. Her brow laden with worries. Gursaran came up to her, 'Shall we start preparing for tomorrow's departure? There are important matters to attend to, back home ...'

'Postpone it for a couple of days,' she was disturbed but not daunted, 'We can't just leave everything midway and go.'

'Cancel the meetings in both Modern School and City Hall,' he was trying to control the damage, 'And in my opinion, we might as well shift our base from this hotel.'

'Stop it,' she was inflamed by the innuendoes, 'You think we can save ourselves by running away? I have heard he has got posters put up all over the city.'

Chandersen was indulging in a smear campaign against Arti Devi. Caricatures of Arti Devi and JK had sprung up everywhere. Posters were plastered everywhere in the city ridiculing Arti Devi, besmirching her, YOUR VOTE AND MY HEART. Chandersen was pulling out all stops. He orchestrated the entire operation in a way that had the entire constituency up and in arms against Arti Devi. Her effigies were being burnt. Her posters were being torched. And the same people who had cried themselves hoarse for her victory, were now baying for her blood. The tables were finally turning his side.

And Chandersen's temerity knew no bounds. He had his supporters sneak into the hotel and had them plaster the hotel walls with many of these posters.

'Remove them,' JK's fury knew no end, 'No ... not like this ... splash water on them. Get some more people and get them removed at once! How the hell did they get inside the hotel, anyway!'

Arti Devi's car drove into the hotel. She did not even look in JK's direction. A wooden stool blocked her way. JK walked up to the stool, picked it up and smashed it against the wall. The car sped in. JK kept looking at the car disappear in the distance.

The table was properly laid out. But JK knew that Arti Devi would not be coming in for dinner. No, not any more. He kept looking at the dinner laid out at the table and then tried to bury himself in his book but peace was not to be found in the pages of the book that he was reading. He closed his eyes.

'Sahib, at least have something to eat,' Binda understood his pain.

'I am not hungry,' JK slowly opened his eyes, 'You eat and go to sleep. Don't wait for her ,' Binda was trying to deny the truth, but could no longer do so, 'she is not coming.' Binda moved away from him, 'And listen, give me the medicine.'

'Okay!'

JK stared at the ceiling for a moment. He was listless. He picked up the phone and dialed the front desk. Amrit picked up the phone.

'Hello Amrit!'

'Yes?'

'Is everything okay?'

'Yes Sir, all well.'

'Oh, yes, did room service send her dinner up?'

'No Sir, she has not yet returned.'

'She still hasn't come?' he was worried, 'Okay, good night!'

JK kept the phone down to find Binda hovering with the medicines. JK took the medicines and gulped them down with water.

'Shall I go to the hotel once and see for myself?' Binda was as concerned as JK

'There's no need to ... just forget that she is here ...'

Binda looked at him soulfully. JK could not meet his eyes. He stood up and walked away from the living room into his bedroom. He slowly lowered himself onto the sofa and then his eyes fell on a dust-covered album peeping out from under the bedside table. He picked it up and, absent-mindedly, began to leaf through the pages. The acid, from the paper on which the photographs had been hinged, had yellowed them, but the memories were intact. JK was soon navigating through the narrow lanes and by-lanes of yesteryears. In one of those photographs, Arti Devi was combing her long open tresses.

Arti looked at her reflection in the mirror as she straightened her hair with the comb. JK captured her image in the camera enthusiastically, simultaneously urging her to smile for him.

'Ismile bhai ... ismile bhai ... ismile.'

'What is this Ismail Bhai ... Ismail Bhai?'

'Not Ismail Bhai ... but smile bhai ... smile please ... smile.'

JK looked satisfied after taking another picture of Arti's, 'Now this is what I call real photography—gorgeous that you are ... I got two ... gorgeous you in my camera—in the foreground as well as in the background!'

Arti pretended to be really impressed with JK's talent as she moved towards the cupboard and took out a crimson bordered white saree.

'Khadi saree! Where are you planning to go? You have to attend yet another meeting? Again? With your father?'

'I have to go out with Daddy, today.'

'And who will take care of her ... your daughter?'

'Her father, of course!'

'And who will go to work?'

'I am going to work. So, it's your turn to take leave today.'

'Look here, memsahib, it is better that you stay here in the comfort of our home,' JK approached her, 'And look after it. This will not do. You can't go out everyday, leaving the baby

alone. Only yesterday, I came home to find our baby in the neighbour's care... and the day before Binda Kaka was getting flustered looking after her. Here give this saree to me!'

Arti deemed it prudent to keep her quiet though she was not pleased to hear JK vent his anger.

'I have told you many times before and I am saying it again for the umpteenth time. I don't like all this.'

'Then, what exactly does he like?' Arti's father had mixed expressions of anger and irritation on his face, 'I can't understand what he wants to make of you? At that time, I tried to tell you not to get married yet. I tried to drum some sense into your head. I told you that it was not time to get married. You have a bright future and this is the time to struggle, to make something of your life. I asked you to first prove yourself, become somebody, and then get married. But you were crazy about him at the time.' Deep within, he was happy that time had proved him right, 'My god! What a waste of talent! I educated you and trained you to become a barrister. You have brought it all to naught ... you had such a bright future ahead of you ... and you have ruined it completely ... all for the sake of a waiter in the hotel ...'

Arti's gaze was focused on the sweater she was knitting and then she looked up at JK, 'Why don't you give up this job in the hotel?'

JK looked deep into her eyes, trying to gauge what was coming next.

'Why don't you do something else?' she wanted to be heard.

'Like what? What do you think I should do?'

'Anything, anything at all. Daddy can set you up in any field...or, you can even do your own business, if you like.'

JK fixed his gaze on his tie in the mirror, 'Can I ask you something?' and then without waiting for Arti's answer, 'Is this idea yours, or your Daddy's?'

'Daddy... Why would Daddy say that?'

'Then, why...what is your problem?'

'I have no problem. I was only talking of your progress. I haven't said anything wrong, have I? All the women in the Women's Council are wives of high officials. I am the only one ...'

'... who is the wife of a hotelier, isn't it?' his self-respect was at stake.

'Yes, isn't that the truth?'

'And this makes you feel small?'

'There is nothing to feel great about it, is there?'

'So who are you married to anyway ... me or my profession?'

JK did not wait for a reply. He grabbed her arm as she rose, 'Listen, Arti, I know you are the daughter of a rich man and you also nurse ambitions to become a leader. But I am a simple and straightforward man, and I would like to remain so. Always. I had told you all this before marriage, hadn't I?? Now, if you are embarrassed being known as my wife, or feel small for any other reason, then you can, whenever you want to, go back to your great father's home!' he paused for breath, 'There is only one request though ... don't create a scene before going. Just tell me, and I will not stop you!'

JK picked up his jacket and walked out. Arti was left contemplating the sudden turn the conversation had taken.

Binda Kaka had also heard everything, 'Sahib has left without eating his breakfast again?'

Arti took her steam out on him, 'So, what should I do? Run after him with his breakfast?'

'No, bitiya, this is not a good thing to happen everyday.'

Arti started to cry, 'You go and feed him, if you feel for him so much!'

'Look, bitiya, your husband's wish should be your wish...'

'Why?' she had had enough of it, 'He is my husband, not

my boss? I am not a servant in his house that he will turn me out if I don't follow his command. If I were in your place then perhaps I would be insecure ...'

Binda looked deeply hurt by her words, and when he spoke his voice was heavy with emotions, 'Even I am not a servant here! I didn't come here to do a job. I have brought you up, so I gave up your father's home to be with you.'

Binda was muttering to himself as he took the breakfast tray and headed towards the kitchen, 'You cannot throw me out of this house ... this household does not run according to my wishes, but it is my home ... when I don't like it here I will leave ... but as per my will and wish ... you cannot kick me out from here ... Mannu is really small ... I will leave with her the day she gets married ... And then I won't stay in this house of yours!'

An eerie silence greeted JK when he returned home that night. Arti was sitting on the bed fumbling with her knitting needles. JK saw her and pulled a chair near the bed and sat down. He had a newspaper in his hand.

'Listen, I want you to come here ....'

'I'll come after some time,' Arti still pretended to be busy with her work.

JK had a stern expression on his face, 'I have an important matter to discuss. Now, come here at once.'

'Why can't you come here?'

JK was seething in rage, 'Get up ... I said stand! Don't try to become my husband, okay!' JK nearly dragged her to bed and brandished the newspaper in front of her face, 'What is this?'

'What?'

'You can read English, can't you? Read and tell me, how did my name appear on this committee?'

'How do I know?'

'You don't know?'

'Father must have recommended you ...'

'Must have? You don't know?'

'I knew!'

'Then why didn't you tell me? Why didn't you inform me?'

'Now it is not as if he has humiliated you or something! He has made you the Honorary President!'

JK could not suppress his anger any longer, 'Stop this nonsense! With whose permission did you give my name? You ... I hate your bloody politics. I have no need for your fake medals and your hollow honors! I am fine as I am, and I am happy with it.'

Arti had a bitter look on her face, 'You may be happy with yourself, but I feel suffocated in this dingy place!'

JK was more shocked than angered as her insinuation dug him deep, 'What did you say? You feel suffocated here? In this dingy place?? Then why are you still here, rotting away? Go ! Go away from here!'

'I would have gone long ago if I were not worried about Daddy's reputation ...'

'So, you are in this house because of your father's reputation ... not because of this house? You are not here for my sake?' The revelation stunned JK. 'Okay, if you can't leave this house because of your father's reputation then I will get out of your way ... I will go away. You may as well have all the freedom you want! But I will not let even your shadow fall either on my life or on my child's!'

Binda Kaka was bringing tea to their room, but stopped at the door when he heard them.

'I will not even let you know where I am or where I go lest you have any unnecessary regret.'

And JK stormed out of the house.

The Manager of the hotel, JK's boss, looked at his resignation letter, 'What is the matter, JK? What is your problem? Why are you resigning?'

'Nothing, Sir. I think I have just had enough of this place!'

'Don't be silly,' he put his hand on his shoulder, 'Today, you are the Assistant Manager, in a couple of years you will become the Manager. If you give up this job now, you will have to start all over again.'

JK said nothing.

The Manager probed, 'What's the matter? Have you had a fight with your wife?' JK looked away from him.

It is the curse of youth to make rash decisions. Arti Devi made one such decision. And Time conspired in such a way that she could only review the decision an eternity later. She sat on her bed to script a letter to JK.

'Tonight, I may not return home. Maybe, I will never come back. The decision is yours. You had told me not to make a scene, I am not doing anything but I want to say clearly how I feel... if we cannot help each other to progress...'

In the silence of the night, JK could hear a thousand drums beating into his ears. '... then why should we become the cause of each other's failure? You will not like it, but I want to tell you myself, before you read it in tomorrow's paper. I am contesting the Municipal elections. Tomorrow, I will have to file those papers as well on which it would have been better if you had signed. Otherwise, I will have to write that we have been separated forever. Whether or not I come home ... the decision is yours ... Arti'

Aggarwal and his supporters sat dwarfed under a canopy on which hung the huge cut-out of the medicine-bottle, his election symbol. This was Aggarwal's maiden address to his electorate.

A seasoned campaigner on the payroll of Aggarwal was introducing him to the crowd, 'Friends! Aggrawal Sahib's name is not new to you. There is hardly anyone here who does not know him. So far, he has been supporting all those candidates of whom he thought well and who he considered good for his people. But today is a different story. Today, he has lost faith in all of them, all of them lie exposed. And in such a scenario, what must a man like Mr Aggarwal do? What choice does he have but to jump into the arena himself? To come to the rescue of the people of the city?' He paused, giving enough time for Aggarwal to sigh and let his presence and his concern be acknowledged. The man caught his breath and resumed exactly at the point he had left, 'Those people who beseech you and beg your votes, those people, their faces are not unknown to you. They come here, to your town and get involved in love affairs ...'

Aggarwal and his supporters sat in ominous silence on the dais, like a jury out on judgment on the conduct of Arti Devi. Little did he know that he was nothing more than a cog in the scheme of things that Lallu Lal was engineering. Lallu Lal himself stood far away from the probing eyes of Aggarwal, one with the crowd. His khadi bag was slung across his shoulders, slightly weighing his shoulders down. He smiled as he heard the speaker drone on.

'... or those who resort to dirty politics and instigate strikes to create hurdles in the progress of the country. I would like to ask this question ... from not only the opponents, but also from each one of you ...'

That was more than what Lallu Lal had come prepared to listen. He took out an egg from his khadi bag and nudged the man next standing next to him. 'Arrey bhaiye, do you have an egg?'

'No, I don't have any egg.'

'Don't you worry ... I have a plenty!' Lallu Lal wrapped a ten-rupee note on the egg and handed it to him, 'here ... have one!'

'What shall I do with it?' he did not get the hang of the conversation.

'Arre bhaiye, peel the wrapper, stuff it in your pocket and let the egg fly up to the dais—there.' Lallu Lal remained poker-faced. And he moved onto the next person very adroitly taking out another egg and wrapping another ten-rupee note around it. The ten rupee notes put wings onto the eggs and Aggarwal and the men on his dais were soon dressed in egg-yolks. The fun-loving section of the crowd soon capitalized on Lallu Lal's initiative and shoes and stones soon began to rain on the speaker who was trying to make himself heard above the din, 'Friends… listen to me ... friends ...'

But the crowd was not listening, not anymore, and Aggrawal had to leave the stage in a hurry and scramble for his safety.

Aggrawal had never been humbled the way he had been during his election campaign. He was used to people obeying him, pampering his ego. And his first brush with public life had upset every known belief of his. And for all this, he held Lallu Lal responsible because, after all, it was on Lallu Lal's say-so that he had decided to contest the elections in the first place.

'You were saying that the workers are our children,' he was seething in rage, 'but they have turned out to be our fathers.'

'Oh ... the follies and the foibles of the young,' Lallu Lal was harping his new tune, 'they are children, after all . . .a bit naughty, just a tad unpredictable! It is a different age and time, you see.'

'That maybe so ... but we need to put order to the anarchy ... these children ought to be disciplined.' Aggrawal was getting desperate.

'Concede to their demands, and they will come along!' Lallu Lal made his next move.

'What?' Even the thought was unthinkable to Aggrawal, 'You have my bankruptcy in mind or what?'

'So, shall I swing in another deal?' Lallu Lal whispered in an alternative, baiting Aggarwal to jump at it.

'And what may that be?'

'You will have to meet Arti Devi once.'

'What for?'

'For the simple reason that the working class listens to her,' Lallu Lal, the veteran of many elections was at his manipulative best.

'Have you gone mad?' Aggrawal shook his head in utter disbelief, 'She is our main opposition ! Why the hell will she help us?'

'Oh, you know how politics is, it basically works on you-scratch-my-back-I-will-scratch-yours' ... a little push here, a little pull there ... anything goes in politics.' Lallu Lal watched him like a hawk. Either Aggarwal was going to fall for it, or he would revolt. There was no third possibility.

'And if she asks me to step down, then?'

'Then you don't step down! That's it! Stick to your guns!'

'Oh, by the way, tell me something ...'

'Yes?'

'This thing about the Manager? Is it true?'

'I don't know,' what Lallu Lal did not admit, admitted an endless number of possibilities, 'But, one thing is sure... there is no smoke without fire.'

Arti Devi sat on the divan, studying a pending piece of legislation that she was planning to introduce in the Parliament when she was returned victorious in the polls. Lallu Lal knocked at the door and asked for an audience. Arti Devi put the papers aside and took off her glasses,

'You have been busy lately.'

Lallu Lal squatted in front of her, a supplicant in her court, 'Not really ...' he paused, cajoled an entreaty in his voice, 'Something important has come up.' Another pause and then he let the words slip in, 'Aggarwal wants to meet you...'

'Why?'

'The thing is—he's made the mistake of contesting the elections...but now, he wants to quit.'

'Why? Is he tired already?'

'Bored, more like it ... he doesn't know a thing about politics ...'

'So, who asked him to contest the elections?'

Lallu Lal, always the shyster, put up a nice little show, 'God knows who that idiot was to suggest that to him ... but now the ground reality is that he cannot go back to Chandrasen ... there's only one option left for him, to align himself with us ... that is if you are ready to accept him in the fold ...' he let the words dangle in front of Arti Devi.

'And why would I be willing?'

'Where's the harm in meeting up with him? Try meeting him once...if you want the meeting can be arranged here, in the hotel itself.'

'Very well ... so what became of his strike?'

'Once he reaches an agreement with you, an agreement with the workers will follow ... it's just that ...'

'I hope you are not setting him up.' Arti Devi scanned his face for any tell-tale signs of manipulation.

'What are you saying! Why would I do something like that?'

'Just remember Lallu Lalji ...' there was an implicit warning in her voice, 'I hate lies ... a battle is never won with lies! If the electorate needs me, it will vote me into Parliament ... if not, it will throw me out! Just don't play games with the electorate!'

'Don't you worry about anything! I never think on such lowly lines.'

'Don't show me your face ever if I get to know that you have manipulated the voters.'

But Lallu Lal was beyond such cares. The means never mattered to him, only winning did.

Worry had added a few creases to JK's forehead. He leaned against the front desk and looked at Amrit, 'I have just received a telegram. Mannu is coming.'

'Mannu is coming?' Amrit always looked forward to

Mannu's arrival from school. 'When is she coming, Sir?'

'She'll be here by the day after tomorrow, but ... Amrit, do me a favour, try and contact the school in Shimla and ask the Principal to hold her back. Tell her I am coming there to pick her up myself. If she has already left, then find out how she is travelling and where I can meet her. I want to get away from here to avoid this election campaigning. If she comes here in the thick of all this mess, it will be even worse ...'

'I'll find out and let you know.'

'If you get through, inform me. I shall be in my office.'

'Yes, Sir.'

JK took out his cigarette packet, shook a cigarette out and just as he was about to light his cigarette, he noticed the hall being spruced up.

'And, why is the hall decorated? Is there a party today?'

'Yes, Mr Aggrawal is hosting a party—drinks and dinner.'

Liveried waiters carried drinks on polished silver. Aggarwal had spared no expense for the party. Everybody who was anybody in the town was going to be there. Aggarwal himself was in good spirits. He fired his cigar and leaned against the bar and looked at Lallu Lal, 'A lakh or two is nothing ... that's peanuts ... I have spent more than that in the last elections ...'

The waiter brought in his drink. Aggrawal dropped a few cubes of ice in his glass and poured himself a stiff drink from the decanter. Single malt whiskey was his weakness. He raised his glass in salute to Lallu Lal, 'Whiskey?'

'No, thank you.' Lallu Lal did not want to spoil an image cultivated with so much difficulty.

'You say no to good whisky?' Aggrawal just could not believe his ears.

'No, I drink only the medicine for my kidneys!' Lallu Lal showed him his 'medicine' bottle.

A hotel phone kept near the bar rang. Somebody from Shimla wanted to speak with JK. A waiter ushered JK in. He picked the phone, 'Hello.'

The principal from Mannu's school was on the other side of the line.

'Hello, Principal Sahib ... I am JK speaking ... Mannu ... yes ... what ... she has already left ...' JK spoke into the phone and swirled around to lean against the bar. At the other end of the bar he caught glimpse of Lallu Lal and Aggrawal. And of Arti Devi coming down the staircase. 'What time does this train approach Allahabad? That's okay ... I'll find out myself ... thank you ...' He replaced the phone in its cradle and picked up the telephone directory and rummaged its pages for the Railways Enquiry number. He could hear Aggarwal's incessant mindless chatter but ignored it.

And then Aggarwal caught sight of Arti Devi. She was now at the foot of the stairs looking at a file that a party worker had brought in. She looked wonderful in a *jamawar* silk sari. Aggarwal could not take his eyes off her.

'Lallu Lalji, that woman still looks ravishing!' Whiskey had loosened his tongue a bit, ' How can any one blame the poor Manager? Anyone can fall for her.'

JK's ears perked up.

Lallu Lal tried to reign in Aggarwal's vagrant thoughts, 'Listen! She will try and tell you to step down. In my opinion ...'

'Lallu Lalji, if she is ready to lie down then I am ready to step down ...' wanton tongues wander unhindered.

That was more than what JK could stomach. He swung Aggrawal roughly towards him, 'What did you say?'

'Oh ho! So, you are the Manager Sahib! Quite a good catch, I must say!'

Barely had the words come out of his mouth that Aggarwal found JK's hand sting him across his face. The force of the slap staggered him and he fell. JK picked him up from the floor and clutched at his collar.

'You ... bastard!' Aggarwal was not used to be treated in this fashion and he was not going to take this from a lowly hotel manager, 'Who the hell is she to you –your mother?'

'I know what she is to me. And when someone dares to ask me I will tell him,' JK dragged him by the collar towards the hotel entrance, past Arti Devi who had just about entered the hall, and threw him out of his hotel, 'Get the hell out of here, or else ...'

'I will get you,' Aggrawal threatened and shook his fist.

JK turned, walked up to Arti Devi, rage seething inside him, 'Listen. I am no bloody politician. I face things straight up. If someone wants to know my relationship with you ... they better ask me not you ... why do they ask you ... what can you answer them when you yourself do not know if a relationship exists between us not ... and if it does what that relationship is?' The rage was finding voice in words, catapulted from the threshold of expression, 'these low and petty things may be the norm in your politics. There is no place for them in my life. Do you understand?' And having vented his fury, JK walked out on Arti Devi, leaving her alone in the cauldron of her own emotions.

Arti Devi's campaign workers were returning after a hectic day in the villages campaigning for a victory that they knew would now never be theirs. The jeep had broken down, come apart like their own election campaign. Their morale was low. They feared the worst. All their hard work had been in vain. Had been brought to naught by a single act of discretion by their leader. They felt betrayed.

'What are you saying ... today the whole town knows ... tomorrow the whole country will know ...'

'Chhi ... chhi ... such a great leader, and having an affair! That too with the hotel Manager!'

'Do you even know what all the people are blabbering? People will talk. No one can stop them.'

The mood was of general despondency. And even the veteran of many a campaign-wars, master-manipulator, the Lallu Lal himself was without hope. He sat huddled with other party-workers, the results of the elections a foregone conclusion, 'She has screwed it up big this time. Today is the last day of campaigning. Tomorrow, the polling will begin. She has destroyed all that we had worked so hard to achieve.'

Nobody saw Arti Devi stride out of the hotel and get into her car and drive away at break-neck speed. They only noticed her when she swerved at the last moment to avoid banging head-on against JK's car. JK got out of the car. He thought he saw Arti Devi driving the car. A few party workers had collected by now.

'Was that Arti Devi?'

'Yes, but where has she gone?' Gursaran was concerned, 'I can't understand. You know, it is an old habit of hers ... whenever she is upset she just goes out for a drive all by herself.'

'Yes, I know, and I also know that she will have some accident or the other. She has not changed a bit ... the same moods ... the same temperament ... the same impulsive nature. Go, or you will soon hear of an accident ...' JK was filled with apprehensions.

'Lallu Lalji,' Gursaran sprung into action, 'Please send the jeep after her and find out where she has gone?'

'Bhaiye,' nothing could lift Lallu Lal's sunken spirits, 'she has gone ... gone back. What is she to do here? Nothing ... even the possibility of a tamasha has been exhausted. There's only Chandersen in the field. He will have a cakewalk of an election. Lucky man!'

'I am not here to talk about Chandersen!' Chandersen's voice boomed across the maidan. He was confident. Arti

Devi had done his work for him. She had erected her own funeral pyre, had even placed herself on it. His job has been made easy. He was here only to light the match and he could see Arti Devi go up in flames. Charred. Beyond recognition. This was a battle he was not going to lose.

'Forget Chandersen,' the crowd was eating out of his hands, 'Chandersen does not want anything. Not even your votes. Chandersen wants justice ... the people's verdict ... your verdict ...' he tugged at his angavastram, his eyes lit up with the glow of anticipated victory, 'I ask you all to think and decide who encouraged the Manager of the hotel to hit Aggrawal Sahib? On whose instigation did he dare to do this? Then, if I say that there is an illegitimate relationship between these two, am I telling lies? Am I wrong in saying this? In front of this august gathering, from this very dais, I had asked Arti Devi three questions. And we, the public have got no answers. Perhaps, she has forgotten ... she has forgotten the public as well ... but, since today is the last day of public meetings, I would like to reiterate my questions ... if Arti Devi desires she can still give her answers. These questions are not mine, they are the public's ... the public is asking ... the public wants to know what her relationship with that Hotel Manager is? Is this relationship that of a husband and wife, or that of a lover and her beloved's? Or is it merely an efficient Hotel

Manager obliged to cater to all sorts of needs of his customers?'

Chandersen paused and scanned the crowd. His words had homed on their target. The crowd was enraged.

'All those who want to become leaders of the public have to present an exemplary character before the people ... they have a responsibility to behave and to do things by which they can command respect ... and those who don't, fall short of the expectations of the public should get out of the way, out of their lives.' The crowd cheered Chandersen, broke into applause. Thus encouraged, Chandersen began to invoke the old traditions of the country, began to exact his pound of flesh, 'The ancient civilization of India ... the age-old traditions ...' but his words began to lose rhythm ... his voice began to trail off as he caught sight of Arti Devi defying the surge of people making her way to the dais.

Arti Devi walked through the crowd, alone, by herself, slowly winding her way to the dais, 'Speak, go on, speak!'

Chandersen was flustered. This was not how he had scripted this show. Things were beginning to fall apart at the seams.

'Why have you stopped at India's ancient civilization,' there was a strange determination in her voice, 'Why don't you carry on?'

Chandersen, the crowd puller and the crowd-winner was not able to understand what Arti Devi had come here for. He had everything worked out for him but this he had not imagined, this he had not foreseen.

'Why have you become tongue-tied?' she took the microphone in her hand, ignored Chandersen and addressed the baffled gathering, 'I have come to your court of justice, brothers and sisters, not to apologize, but to appeal for justice! Hear me out, and then be my judge and my jury and then, and only then, sentence me ... however harsh your sentence may be I will accept it ... if you think I deserve the most rigorous punishment, so be it,' she fought hard to control the lump that was clawing at her throat. 'You want to know what this Manager of Hotel Ashiana is to me? What his relationship with me is? My esteemed opponent has asked some questions in very harsh words. I would like to know how he would feel if his wife was asked the same question about him?'

Chandersen was aghast as he heard this.

'If he is so interested in my private life, he could have asked me, and I would have introduced him to the hotel manager and said here meet JK ... he is my husband!'

Far away, JK was standing in the crowd, listening to her.

'Yes, yes, I say it with pride. He is my husband, and if it

is a sin to meet my husband, then I stand before you, guilty as accused. If it is a sin to go to your husband's house, then I stand before you, guilty as accused. If it is a sin to hold your husband's hand, after years of separation then I stand before you guilty as accused.' Repressed emotions were taking their claim on her voice. It began to quiver, nearly choking on her tears. She turned her head away from the crowd.

Her words brought JK on the dais, he came and held her arm, 'Arti.'

She looked up and saw him, ' Good you came here. . .and took hold of me,' she found her strength in him, and slowly, she turned to face the sea of people again. 'Here I stand, your accused, your culprit beseeching you for your verdict,' she paused, 'Twelve long years ago, we both got married to each other ... we have a daughter who studies in Shimla ... that's all there is to the story of my personal private life. . .and this is what does not meet with the approval of these great leaders of yours . . .they called it illegitimate and dirty ... They've reduced me and my relationship to unpalatable caricatures plastered across the walls of this city, dragged me into distasteful headlines across their newspapers...' she laboured for breath, 'how was I to bring myself to tell you that I had abandoned my husband, my daughter for all those years, for ten long years ... abandoned them so that I could be with you. For all those ten years I have been with you ... sharing your joys and your sorrows ... I have paid a huge price to stay with you, amongst you all ... the time that I owed to my husband and my daughter, I gave it all—to you. Let me ask you. . .what kind of woman wouldn't want to be with her husband after ten long years ... to know the life that they were supposed to have spent together, how they have spent it separately ... I ask you with folded hands. . . please do not vote for me ... I don't want to stay in politics. I want to go back ... to my home ... to my husband ... to my daughter. I don't want anything else from you. Please give me your blessings if you can, get me justice ... and if you still think I am guilty then punish me, by all means!'

The crowd was stupefied. Even Lallu Lal's eyes filled with tears. JK put his arm around her shoulder and took her away through the crowds.

A crowd has the innocence and naïveté of a child. A crowd does not nurse grievances. A crowd is not malicious. If a few words can make it sizzle in anger, a few words can also make it see reason.

The maidan was soon rent with cries of 'Long live Arti Devi'.

Arti Devi ki jai!

Arti Devi ki jai!

The crowd had exonerated Arti Devi of all the charges.

‘According to the latest reports it is learnt that Mr Aggrawal has stepped down in favour of Chandersen, hence the chances of his victory have increased. Shrimati Arti Devi ... ’ As she heard her name, Arti Devi switched off the radio. They were in JK’s car.

JK looked at her, ‘Why ... why did you switch the radio off?’

He was greeted with a wall of silence. Arti looked at him and then looked away.

‘It’s a good thing that you are coming home,’ there was no tremor in his voice, ‘but don’t do it because you have lost the elections. Your defeat can never be my victory. I don’t want to see you defeated. Ever. Neither at home nor outside. Whatever you do, do it with faith and confidence.’

Arti just kept looking at JK.

'According to the latest reports the status of the three contestants is as follows: Shri Gul Sher Ahmad Khan ... total votes – 1203, Shri Chandersen – 50735, Shrimati Arti Devi – 55940. Arti Devi is leading her closest rival by 5202 votes.' Arti Devi leaned towards the radio. The newsreader added an update, 'According to the final tally Arti Devi is leading by a margin of 48,020 votes. Now her victory is almost certain.'

JK stood across the threshold, a towel across his shoulder. They looked at each other— unwilling, and yet forced to acknowledge that their little time together was now over.

The rotors of the helicopter whizzed to life. Arti Devi stood under their sweeping arc with folded hands, bidding adieu to her campaign workers. She walked up to Lallu Lal and thanked him.

'If I am alive, I will serve you in the next elections as well. Namaste!'

She moved towards JK. JK did not know how to say a goodbye, 'You have to go. I understand. You must complete what you have started. I want to see you victorious in everything you do ... always ...'

'Mannu is coming tomorrow. If only I could stay for one more day, I could have met her.'

'I will ask her to visit you before she returns to the hostel. She will stay with you for a few days then you can take her to the hostel.'

Arti's eyes welled up with tears. She bent down to touch his feet. And they both moved towards the chopper. She tried to wipe her tears with the pallu of her sari, but the tears kept flowing.

She climbed into the helicopter and strapped herself to the seat. JK held her hand, reluctant to let go. But finally, he had to let her hand slip out of his.

Their eyes met. A part of her life reflected in his eyes. He knew he did not need to tether her to his life. There was pride in her victory. And she knew that he would always be a part of her life even if they could not be together.

The helicopter lifted itself into the air and JK stood below, rooted to the spot, till it became a tiny speck in the sky.